SHERLOCK HOLMES

By the same author:

The British Hearse and the British Funeral, Book Guild
Publishing, 2011

SHERLOCK HOLMES

The Missing Earl and Other New Adventures

*A selection of cases published by arrangement with
the estate of the late Doctor Watson, M.D.*

N.M. Scott

Book Guild Publishing
Sussex, England

First published in Great Britain in 2012 by
The Book Guild Ltd
Pavilion View
19 New Road
Brighton, BN1 1UF

RONDO	15/01/2012
F	£ 16.99
COALIS	

Printed in Great Britain by
CPI Group (UK) Ltd, Croydon, CR0 4YY

A catalogue record for this book is available from
The British Library

ISBN 978 1 84624 647 0

In memory of Uncle Harold

Contents

1

The Haversham Jackdaw

On New Year's Day in that bitter winter of 1890, Holmes and myself were walking down Baker Street from the Oxford Street end. Despite sporadic scatterings of cinders, the pavements of the metropolis were icy and treacherous underfoot. It had started snowing again and there was a fierce northerly wind. Much to our amusement – for mirth has a warming way about it – an elderly gentleman upon the other side of the street was bracing himself to fend off the swirling sleet with his umbrella when, quite unexpectedly, due to a particularly strong gust – the shaft parted company with the handle!

The poor fellow grimly held on and watched aghast whilst the rest of his brolly rose into the air and floated across the street like a gigantic crow. It came crashing down and proceeded to slide along the icy pavement as though it were on skates.

Holmes, evidently enjoying himself, ran after it, managed to trap the wayward brolly beneath his shoe and energetically stamped upon the thing a couple of times – presumably to kill it.

'Why, thank you, Sir,' said the gentleman, as he

came puffing across the road to claim his other half.

'You shall have to get it repaired,' said I. 'There is a place along Wimpole Street – do you know it?'

'I fear I shall have to throw it away, Sir,' said he, carefully examining the twisted spokes and rent canvas. 'But I am nonetheless extremely grateful to your friend here. I should not have fancied being taken to court over the loss of an eye or worse. By the way, does either of you gentlemen live hereabouts?'

'Yes, we do – whose place are you after?'

'I am looking for a Mister Sherlock Holmes,' he replied. 'I've tried at least three addresses so far – all of them up at the metropolitan end – and not managed to find him, yet!'

'Then, you need look no further,' said I, 'for by way of coincidence, Mister Sherlock Holmes is the very man who has just rescued your umbrella!'

'Thank God,' said he, evidently much relieved. 'My name is Reginald Canty, Sir, and I am a retired accountant from Surrey.'

'Well, Mister Canty,' my friend said, adjusting his scarf, 'I take it that whatever led you to stray from your hearth on such a brazenly cold morning as this must be of some importance! The number is 221b, by the way!'

The snow had started to fall heavily and we scrambled into a cab and followed the main artery of traffic back to our lodgings.

Canty was a likeable enough character. He possessed the dignified, reserved manner of an ex-City man, hardened by and slightly cynical from decades of commuting. Bright green eyes held you in a steady gaze and a square, determined jaw spoke of a lifetime of responsibility concerning banking procedures and company balance sheets.

Holmes and myself settled back in our armchairs in front of the bright, cheery fire and listened with considerable interest as Canty explained why he had troubled to commute from Haversham to seek out the advice of my colleague.

'There has been a New Year's Eve burglary, Mister Holmes,' said he. 'In fact, I regret to say, several of them!'

'Hum – and you were one of the casualties, I take it?'

'That is correct,' he replied, 'and worse – I have no inkling how the thief broke into my house and still less how he actually managed to escape. The matter does not simply rest there, however, for this morning I received a summons from my neighbour, Philip Lamb, a bank manager, and discovered to my surprise that his own house had been burgled and he, in turn, had been informed that the house opposite belonging to Stanley Rogers, a broker, had received a dose of the same!'

'And, pray, exactly what was stolen?'

'Jewellery, Sir. My wife lost her diamond tiara, a ruby necklace and several rings, although strangely enough, none of my own personal effects were touched and this proved to be the case with Lamb and Rogers.'

'Did you inform the police about the theft?'

'I did not wish to have my name or that of my wife manufactured in print and used to enliven innumerable headlines and sell newspapers. Rogers and Lamb felt likewise – the matter has not been discussed outside our circle. We celebrated the New Year and our servants joined us at midnight to partake of the customary toast. At well past one my wife decided to go upstairs to bed. I was about to join her but thought it prudent to remind Matthews – a sincere and obliging fellow and altogether one of the most sensible domestics we have ever employed – that one of the windows in the conservatory required battening. Shortly after, my wife gave out the most fearful scream.'

'And where did your wife normally keep her jewellery?'

'In a Chippendale cabinet beside her dressing table.'

'And it was unlocked?'

'Certainly! I mean, a lady does not expect to have her boudoir suddenly broken into! Although it was still bitterly cold, I remembered no snow had fallen since the previous afternoon – thus, after comforting my wife and leaving a servant with her, I decided to take Matthews, together with the dogs and a lantern, and search every inch of my property. I was determined that if the thief had left behind any tell-tale evidence of his night's work, I should be the first to discover it! Outside, the cylindrical ridge of snow running along the length of the stone walling bordering my garden remained unbroken. I therefore surmised that no one had attempted to climb over it.'

4

'How perceptive of you!' remarked my colleague, with a twinkle in his eyes, smoking his pipe and glancing out at the sleet pattering against the window pane.

'Oh, I have a weakness for crime novels and the like, Mister Holmes, and thought I might be able to put the knowledge I had gleaned to practical use!'

'Ha! Please don't keep us in suspense, Mister Canty. Perhaps you could tell us about the prints you discovered on the lawn.'

'Well, I was about to get to that,' said the retired accountant, becoming overtly puffed up, unaware of my companion's humorous turn of mind and, no doubt, imagining he was about to follow in the steps of Poe and produce some masterly oracle of detection.

'The lawn was covered in snow to a depth of, I should say, about a foot. All I could discern from its frozen surface were the prints of my dogs and various species of bird. The moonlit path seemed to be very much the same as I remembered it the evening before.

'Matthews, I think, visited the bird table on a few occasions. No one else – apart from the dogs – had ventured across it for days. I then turned to face the house and perceived the window ledges had not been trampled on, if a ladder had been used – I could find no sign of one, anywhere. We possess a long ladder with two stages of rungs and yet nobody had been near it.'

'My dear Watson, from what Mister Canty has told us so far, this portends to be a most singular case. We have three houses each in close proximity to the other – granted, the New Year festivities allow a considerable leeway for the burglar, however, you mentioned you keep dogs, Mister Canty?'

'Indeed, we all do,' he said with some surprise. 'My spaniel barks at the slightest provocation and Lizzie, the Scotch terrier, although inclined to be of a more placid temperament, will join in whenever the opportunity arises. Stanley Rogers keeps a black Labrador, Lamb, a collie!'

'Haversham's in Surrey, isn't it?' said Holmes. 'Do many trains run there on New Year's Day?'

'A normal service – trains leave Victoria on the half-hour every hour, passing through Croydon. However, bad weather might have affected the times, you know, frozen points, else a portion of line blocked by snow.'

'Then I suggest we forfeit the excellent wild duck Mrs Hudson was preparing for lunch, Watson, and take a cab straightaway to Victoria.'

We arrived at Haversham at just past two. The train was late for the signals were working very badly and there were intermittent delays along the line. Canty lived in a pleasant wooded cul-de-sac on the outskirts of Haversham, not far from Deacons Common and the Swan Inn. The area was fairly well-to-do, with most properties belonging to retired City accountants, stockbrokers and the like.

In pointing out the houses belonging to Henry Lamb and his neighbour, Stanley Rogers, Canty made it clear that each had been designed by the quirky Scandinavian architect, Svenson, and this accounted for the peculiar mixture of styles – best described as a combination of 'European' and British 'medieval'. For instance, the front of Canty's residence was built like an Alpine hunting-lodge, with a round Norman turret at either end, whereas to confuse matters the back incorporated the traditional Tudor facade of rosy brickwork, many timbers and latticed windows. This was not so bizarre to the Englishman's eye as it might at first appear, for the bad weather enhanced the aspect of these dwellings wonderfully, and in this landscape one could quite easily have been about to test the slopes of the Tyrol or encounter a herdsman with his reindeer!

We were greeted beneath the snow-covered porch by Mrs Canty and her two dogs, and shown into a large, airy drawing room, comfortably furnished and with a fire blazing merrily in the grate. By necessity we all stood in front of it, warming our freezing hands.

'How kind of you to come,' said Mrs Canty. 'My trinkets I suppose, would fetch little at auction, but I attach great sentimental value to them. None could ever be replaced you see – Gloria Lamb is heartbroken over the affair. Her diamond engagement ring and a pair of her mother's matching ruby ear-rings are missing, and yet, why should this thief choose to ignore my husband's wallet, his gold repeater and cuff links? There was some valuable plate in the next room also.'

Holmes smiled, lighting his pipe and tossing the match into the flames, his eyes bent low upon the glow of the fire.

'I think I can offer a plausible explanation,

Madam,' said he. 'Perhaps the burglar was only interested in gem stones?'

'Why, I had never thought of it quite like that, Mister Holmes,' she confided, picking up her Scotch terrier and patting its head affectionately.

'A jackdaw of sorts?' I interjected.

'Yes, a very apt description, my dear Watson,' said my colleague, tapping the stem of his pipe upon the mantelpiece. He then turned to Reginald Canty, who sat by the fire, a golden-haired spaniel curled at his feet, listening to all that had been said with a keen interest.

'Could I borrow your ladder? It will only be for a half-hour or so.'

'The ladder?' he exclaimed.

'I wish to climb on to the roof. What about you, Watson? Are you game?'

'Certainly,' said I, putting on my gloves.

'Then I shall ask Matthews to fetch it,' said Canty, ringing for the servant.

'Capital! I shall start with the Lambs' house next door and work my way round,' my companion remarked, getting ready to leave.

Simplicity and utility were evidently in Svenson's mind when he designed the Lambs' house, for it could quite easily have passed for a customs post on the Swiss frontier – less hybrid than Canty's dwelling, it possessed a high shelf or platform on the roof, apparently once designated to become a glass-domed observatory but which, according to Canty, never materialised on account of its prohibitive cost and the widespread criticism the project received from the local population. Great icicles hung from the porch and the glow from the lantern made the snow shimmer like polished diamonds, for a hard frost had set in.

Philip Lamb answered the door in his dressing gown. He was a thin, wiry individual, with swept-back silver hair and spectacles. His beady eyes examined us over a large, hawkish nose.

'You are Mister Sherlock Holmes, I take it?'

'I am. And this is my companion, Doctor Watson – your wife took things rather badly, I hear?'

'I am afraid that is the case. Are you coming in? My wife is in the music room at present, so you shan't disturb her. I presume you do want to see the bedroom?' he said, looking suspiciously at Matthews and the long ladder he was carrying.

'I don't think that will be necessary, Mister Lamb. However, I should like to get on to your roof, if I may?'

'My roof!' The bank manager seemed taken aback by this request.

'Perfectly so – as you can see, Mister Canty has kindly supplied a ladder from next door for that same purpose!'

'Surely you are not implying that the thief, somehow, managed to scale the side of my house, Mister Holmes? Why, he should require the physiognomy of a multi-taloned insect, Sir!'

'I doubt whether the thief was transmuted into a fly, Mister Lamb, though I grant you he has a most ambidextrous mind. If I were you, I should shut the door – you'll catch the death of cold standing out here!'

Lamb stuck his glasses firmly upon his nose, gave

my friend a quizzical, uncertain stare and closed his door. Without delay we went round to the side of the house and the ladder was leaned against the wall and manoeuvred into position by Matthews.

'This is preposterous, Watson!' said Holmes, gazing up at the wall. 'See how the blanket of snow on the ledge and timbers remains undisturbed.'

'We shall need some sort of light up there,' said I.

'I have the very thing, Sir, a dark lantern. I took the precaution of bringing it along with me,' said the manservant.

'You excel yourself, Matthews!' said Holmes, snatching the lamp and clambering up the ladder.

I eventually managed to climb over some parapets and scramble onto the roof and there I could vaguely discern the bent figure of Holmes, his hawk-like features lit up by the gleam of the lamp, poring over the snow with his magnifying lens.

'I do not possess a spirit level, Watson, but tell me what you make of the window to the loft, will you?'

'Why, both sliding sections do not run true with the sill,' said I.

'Yes, and the window frame is only lightly pinned in and should lift away easily from the wall with the aid of a chisel. You will observe how the lime-based mortar has not been mixed properly and the brick-nogging around the window needs re-pointing!'

'Thanks to the British speculative builder the house-breaker has no need of a glass-cutter these days!' said I, incredulously. 'He simply removes the entire window – glass panels and all!'

'And replaces it afterwards – yes, that's how he got in, Watson, and yet I cannot fathom how on earth he got up here in the first place.'

Suddenly, his bewildered expression was transposed to one of glee. He rushed over to one of the parapets and, scraping away the fresh layer of fallen snow with his hand, sifted what lay beneath through his fingers and placed something in his pocket.

'Ha – this fellow is certainly no ordinary lark, Watson!'

'I think it's about time this jackdaw had his wings clipped a little,' said I.

'Yes – we must get down from this great height and search out his nest, for I am certain it is there we shall find the missing gems.'

We left Matthews to retrieve the ladder and went straight away next door where Canty and his wife were both sat with their dogs, anxiously awaiting our return.

'Do you know of Colonel Bradstock-Hume?' said Holmes, warming his frozen hands by the fire.

Canty thought for a moment and lit his cigar. 'Do you mean the engineer responsible for the Lyneham Bridge?'

'That is the very man,' replied Holmes.

'Not personally, although I believe he is something of a local celebrity and lives over in Radstone at Compton Old Hall, Mister Holmes – just a few stops down the line from Haversham.'

'I see. Well, I should like to pay this Colonel Bradstock-Hume a visit.'

'I think you shall find him away at present – in Tunisia working on a dam.'

'Are there many trains to Radstone?'

'One train every hour up until midnight, but I can assure you, Mister Holmes, your visit to Radstone would be a wasted one for according to the *Surrey Gazette* the Colonel will be away for several weeks.'

The train to Radstone was already standing in the platform when we arrived at the station. We hurriedly collected our tickets and went straight away to a waiting carriage.

'Good gracious Holmes,' said I, as we each lit a cigarette. 'What has Colonel Bradstock-Hume got to do with all this? Has the thief somehow managed to conceal his hoard upon the Colonel's property? If so, I'm damned if I know how you discovered it.'

'It is the Colonel himself that interests me, Watson. He is a keen sportsman and, it so happens, I recall reading about one of his exploits in the *Telegraph*, last year.'

'Has he fallen on hard times and needs the swag to see him through? I suppose he'll get a few hundred pounds for his night's haul – if he's lucky – that is!'

'Oh, he is wealthy enough.'

'Then what was his motive?'

'It is elementary, my dear Watson. The Colonel believed he could commit the perfect crime and get away with it. However, our jackdaw's wings are about to be clipped and I have not the slightest intention of allowing him to get off lightly!'

We alighted at Radstone station and immediately went and enquired of the porter the exact whereabouts of Compton Old Hall and were accordingly directed down a steep hill. It was a frosty night and the road remained an unbroken white line – a gleaming icy surface, pavements frozen and hedgerow trees over-arched with snow. At the bottom of the hill I observed a large country house, partly disguised by trees, its gabled roof glittering under the softening light of the moon. This was evidently Compton Old Hall – the residence of Colonel Bradstock-Hume.

We arrived at the lodge gates and were trudging up the drive when a light glimmered and a burly individual emerged from the shadows of the entrance porch holding a lamp. I heard a barn owl screeching from the tall oaks bordering the park, followed by a low whistle, and instinctively reached for my service revolver, for out of the blackness two large and ferocious Dobermans came bounding towards us.

'Come away, Rex!' a voice then shouted coarsely. 'And you, Salter! Come back, I say at once!'

The dogs obediently turned on their heels and went trotting back to their master, no doubt happy for the exercise.

'You, there, Sir!' the figure shouted, pointing in my direction. 'You are trespassing on my property! Kindly leave the grounds and take your friend there with you!'

'I presume that it is Colonel Bradstock-Hume of Compton Old Hall I have the pleasure of addressing?' said Holmes, with a most reposeful air.

The Colonel, whose massive stature was daunting, trudged over to greet us. The dogs circled about his great ham-thighs, their eyes glinting menacingly.

'Ah, now I see you are both gentlemen.' He held out his hand. 'I apologise for my rough manner. At first I took you to be a couple of jemmy-bashers come to set about my fine plate and blow my safe, though I confess I have never met either of you before. Are you come about the Istanbul contract?'

'I have come about a burglary in Haversham, Colonel,' said Holmes, sternly.

The engineer's jaw dropped and he instantly averted his gaze from my companion's, preferring to look at the ground instead.

'You are the police, I take it?' he muttered.

Holmes, with a thin smile upon his lips, deliberately allowed Bradstock-Hume to ruminate over his guilty secret for a while and after about fifteen seconds had elapsed said quietly: 'No, we are not.'

The relief on the engineer's face was evident. 'I think you'd both better come inside and share a blast of fire.'

We passed up a snow-covered flight of steps and were led into a warm, spacious oak-panelled room filled with the dense reek of cigar smoke. There was a desk covered with the detailed plans of various engineering projects the Colonel had undertaken and we waded across rolls of drawing paper, large reference works, set squares and the like, to a pair of handsome Jacobean chairs, set either side of the fireplace.

'Do take a seat!' said he.

He poured us a glass of whisky and soda each, and lounging in front of the hearth with his dogs said matter-of-factly: 'You will observe, gentlemen, that I possess a number of glass-sided cabinets containing all manner of intricate brass models, supplied with working parts and built by myself, mostly for exhibitions. There is an American Wild West locomotive and a fireman's pump engine. Place a penny in the slot and the wheels shall start spinning, else, a piston rod gyrate back and forth.'

Rex and Salter lay stretched on a large Turkey rug, watching their master with gleaming, baleful eyes by the light of the flickering coal fire.

'Ingenious!' Holmes replied. 'But, I have no pennies and besides, more pressing matters must needs be seen to!'

'What are your names?' asked the Colonel.

'Sherlock Holmes,' replied my friend, 'and this is my colleague, Doctor Watson.'

'Indeed, I should be interested to learn why on earth you chose to waste your time – and mine – by coming out here on a freezing night to discuss these burglaries in Haversham, Mister Holmes.'

'Burglaries – did I mention more than one? I don't believe I did!' said my colleague with a whimsical smile.

'Oh, I read something about it in the *East Surrey Chronicle*,' he answered in a slovenly way.

'Wasn't it the *Surrey Gazette*?'

'Of course!'

'Well, that's a queer thing, because the matter was deliberately kept discreet and no article appeared in any of the papers. I shall speak plainly, Colonel Bradstock-Hume. I have come here to Compton Old Hall tonight because I know you to be the thief – come now man, admit it! You have already committed a prize blunder.'

'Nonsense!' replied the Colonel, irately, but before he could say another word, Holmes put up his hand and waved all objections aside.

'And I have more than a grain of evidence to prove it!' Holmes came and stood behind the Colonel's chair, placed his hand into his pocket and retrieved a damp ball of fine-grained sand of a deep reddish colour, which he carefully sifted through his long bony fingers and spread over the armrest.

'Excellent ballast – wouldn't you agree, Colonel?'

The proud soldier slumped back in his chair and grew very pale.

'One of your sacks was most likely damaged when you made your descent and landed upon the observatory platform. Watson, come over here, will you? I have something to show you.'

I joined my colleague by the window and as I glanced out of the black pane, there, in the park behind the Colonel's house, I was amazed to see an air balloon, with taut ropes and grapnel hooks holding it to the ground and sacks of ballast dangling from the basket suspended beneath.

'Masterly! If Charlie Peace were alive I am sure he would play his fiddle for you, Colonel!'

'I am glad you seem so amused, Mister Holmes. I am wondering whether my little aeronautical adventure has ended on a sour note, though I'm damned if I haven't met an equal in you! Tell me, Sir, am I for the county jail or what is it worth to you and your fine friend here to keep me out? I am wealthy enough to offer you a good envelope each, for your trouble.'

16

'That will not be necessary, Colonel. You are acquainted with the Scandinavian architect Frederik Svenson, I take it?'

'Ah, I see where this is leading, Mister Holmes. Yes, he seeks my advice from time to time about structural problems arising from his often complex and radical designs.'

'And, I recall you collaborated together on the much criticised Stenbäck Opera House in Helsinki?'

'Fredi owns a ferro-concrete bungalow, designed by himself, at the western end of Lake Utsjoki. I stayed with him when I was working on the plans for the opera house and it was there, whilst enjoying a Finnish bath, that he slung a tub of water over the hot stones and asked me the following question: "Do you know of the Haversham development?" I told him I lived nearby and had read about it in the Society's journal and he, thereafter, boasted that all three of the houses he had designed were burglar proof, for he employed a unique system of shutters and all the locks and catches were manufactured to his own specification. I warned him not to underestimate the ingenuity of the English criminal class, for invariably their motto was "Where there's a will there's a way" and, to a perpetual egoist like himself, this was tantamount to being challenged to a duel. He immediately laid down odds, and hefty ones they were too I might add, that, no thief could possibly accomplish such a thing. Being fond of a bet, I decided to have a go myself.

'To overcome the problem of locks and latches, upon my return to this country I paid a visit to the Guildford firm of White and Perry, who originally carried out the work, and managed to obtain some useful information. Over a pipe, Perry – a near-neighbour of mine – showed me the plans and pointed out that in order to cut corners and thereby make an enormous profit, amongst other areas of skimped workmanship certain of the attic windows were not provided with outer shutters, nor were the frames, to his knowledge, set properly into the wall. They were high up and awkwardly placed, but the unique pitch of the roofs and, in one case, the redundant observatory platform, would make the task of burglaring the houses much easier than I had at first envisaged.

'Svenson did not wish to part with his money easily and one of his impossible provisos stated that the burglary must take place when the houses were occupied. Another was that all three should be burgled together!

'The more I thought about it, the less hopeful I became, and then I struck upon the bright idea of incorporating my hot-air balloon into the scheme of things. Flying has always been a passion of mine and I thought perhaps, with room to manoeuvre, I might conceivably vault over the trees, land on the observatory platform and then hop over to the others. The last week in December, I telegraphed Svenson and arranged to meet him here at my house on New Year's Eve. He accompanied me on my criminal escapade as overseer, to make sure fair play was in order, and, as a consequence, departed for Ostend this morning with his tail between his legs – several thousand pounds, the poorer – having lost his bet, but with a good deal more respect for the Englishman than ever he owned before our little adventure!'

'I presume you were about to make another trip tonight and return the missing jewellery?'

'It was to have been my hundredth ascent, however, not wishing to tempt fate a second time, I should have landed on Deacons Common at midnight and legged it across the woods from there. I have in my possession three separate packets, each containing the missing gems. I had intended to place them on the doorsteps, to be reclaimed by the ladies tomorrow morning!'

'Whilst I appreciate your verve and tenacity in seeking to aspire to the perfect crime, you failed to appreciate the feelings of others.'

'You'll inform the police, then, Mister Holmes?' said he, realising for the first time the full gravity of the situation.

'No, although you shall have some honest explaining to do when we return to Haversham – for these ladies are to be your judge and jury, Colonel Bradstock-Hume!'

The old gentleman frowned. 'Very well then, if it is to be a "petticoat court" I must face, so be it. I should prefer to take my chances there than with a real one!'

'The recovery of the stolen jewellery and an extremely generous donation to the ladies' favourite poor charity might help swing the balance in your favour. I shall, of course, accompany you to the hearing with Doctor Watson here, who is himself a very lenient judge of character!'

The Colonel seemed much relieved. 'I suppose we had better catch the train – there is one in ten minutes upon the hill.'

'Oh, a train!' said Holmes, somewhat caustically, 'you disappoint me!'

'Ah, you wish to survey the old market town of Haversham from a great height?' answered the Colonel, laughing heartily. 'There is nothing quite like a flight in an air balloon. The sensation is most agreeable and complimentary to the digestive organs, Doctor Watson!'

And so we flew in an air balloon, and drifted upon the air currents for a quarter hour until we began our descent and landed on Deacons Common. I was disappointed that our journey had come to an end so soon, for the view of the Surrey hills from that great height with the lights of the houses glittering like diamonds beneath was truly magnificent to behold.

2

The Amorous Surgeon

In the second week of November 1895 I enjoyed a chance encounter with my friend, Mister Sherlock Holmes. It was a recital of Mendelssohn at the Wigmore Hall. My friend, who unbeknown to me, sat behind my seat, tapped my shoulder and in the most cordial terms proposed that I might leave my Paddington practice in the capable hands of another for a few days, and join him at his diggings in Baker Street.

The weather was foul and the fogs particularly severe that year. The streets of the metropolis were blanketed by the aforementioned impenetrable and insufferable contagion that daily blighted the lives of its inhabitants. That very morning I had attended some poor devil – a clerk from Threadneedle Street – run over by a hansom and critically injured, barely a hundred yards or so from my own doorstep.

The following day, once again in the cosy and familiar surroundings of my old rooms in Baker Street, I seated myself before the fire and lit a cigar. I knew already that my colleague was wholly preoccupied with the recent outrages that had shocked London society. He indicated the pile of crumpled morning papers and taking down his Persian slipper from the mantelpiece, filled his pipe with tobacco.

'Well, my dear Watson, you have no doubt perused over the morning editions. What do you make of the affair, so far?'

'It is a distressing business,' said I, 'although I take exception to the way some Fleet Street editor has, in order to maintain a vast circulation of newspapers, perversely dubbed the perpetrator of these shocking crimes "the amorous surgeon"!'

'Perfectly natural that a man of your medical background should find the title irksome!' my friend conceded. 'Nonetheless, it is a very apt one – to recount: the first person to fall into his clutches was Miss Adelaine Pardoe, a lady-in-waiting to the Duchess of Roxborough, that old autocratic empress to whom the fashionable young things of London flock. Her town house in Cheyne Walk is a favourite social venue for poets and other literary figures, I believe. After spending the evening with her friend, the debutante Lucinda Welles, who lives in a pleasant mews apartment in Sloane Street, Belgravia, Miss Pardoe took a stroll along the Chelsea Embankment. It was foggy and she had not walked very far when someone rushed from behind and placed a handkerchief over her face. In Miss Pardoe's own words, taken from a statement she made shortly before her death – and I shall quote them here, she says: "The pungent odour made me feel all at once revolted, but afterwards such a feeling of euphoria overwhelmed me – I began to hum a popular music hall tune."'

I laughed. 'Yes, women have been known to sing on the operating table! Ether or chloroform would produce such a euphoric state of mind. After what must have been a considerable lapse of time – for it was nearly dawn – a constable found her lying unconscious on a bench by the King's Road. Help was immediately summoned and it was discovered that one of Miss Pardoe's legs had been amputated just below the knee. The stump was expertly bandaged and a silk garter – such as a gentleman might present to his lady friend or a mistress – had been slipped over it,' said I.

'And, yet, her personal physician issued a statement to the effect that there had never, in his opinion, ever been anything remotely wrong with her leg. The circulation was perfectly normal. No past report of tumour, lesions, gangrene, abnormality of the bone, fractures, or any other such medical prognosis. In plain language, my dear Watson, her leg had been amputated just for the sport of it! That same morning she died, her frail constitution being unable to withstand the shock, and Scotland Yard was duly informed of the incident.'

'The amputation was performed at some unknown location. A "first class job", as the coroner who performed the autopsy later put it. Perhaps it was a medical student playing a prank?' said I.

'Perhaps,' Holmes remarked, lighting his pipe and stretching his long legs in front of the hearth. 'Anyhow, another notable personage to fall victim to this fellow's queer sense of humour is none other than Lady Stoker-Brant, a distant cousin to the Queen and the widow of the famous explorer, mountaineer and military historian, Major General Sir James Arthur Stoker-Brant, who also resides in Cheyne Walk – incidentally! She is, at present, convalescing at Saint George's. The injuries are singular in the fact that they are virtually identical to those sustained by her predecessor. Have you a couple of hours to spare, Watson? If so, I suggest we might take a cab to Saint George's and interview her.'

At the hospital, in the presence of her personal physicians, Sir Arthur Newton and Doctor Perigold-McFarlen, my companion, certainly aware from his own background and experience of the Court etiquette required, however informally in such circumstances, stood stiffly before the Grand Dame, removed his hat and bowed briefly.

He then sat beside her bed and asked her a few questions.

'And pray, why were you walking along the Embankment at such a late hour?'

'Merely to take a little air, Sir! It is a habit of mine I suppose – my town house being so close to the river.'

'And yet you were surely aware that an atrocious crime had been committed a few days earlier along that same stretch of the Embankment?'

'My neighbour, the Duchess of Roxborough, mentioned it to me certainly, although I had little personal acquaintance with this Adelaine Pardoe.'

'Were you not discouraged?'

'Not particularly!'

'And you went out alone?'

She nodded. 'Mister Holmes, it never occurred

to me that this "amorous surgeon" or whoever should concern himself with one of my own class!' Lady Stoker-Brant was a litigious woman, proud of her rank and high station in life and did not choose to mince words. 'Servants are, of course, another matter, Mister Holmes!'

I hardly considered a lady-in-waiting as part of the 'below stairs' establishment but my colleague, nonetheless, allowed her slight eccentricities to amuse him.

'You will appreciate it was dark and foggy. I crossed the Grosvenor Road and was progressing along the Embankment a hundred yards or so from my town house in Cheyne Walk. I recall the lights of Battersea Bridge in the foreground and the pilot lantern of a passing wherry, my attention being wholly centred upon the river.'

'Do you recall having heard anything remotely suspicious? Footsteps for instance?' said I.

Lady Stoker-Brant, her eyes those of a young girl, bright and keenly intelligent and of a rich violet hue, momentarily gazed upon me and I felt the thrill of old world aristocracy enter my veins.

'I heard a man's voice – a cockney!'

My friend, who during this interview had found it increasingly difficult to maintain his rather frigid expression, burst into a peal of laughter.

'Ha! A cockney indeed!' said he, slapping his knee, evidently much intrigued by her ladyship's haughty and ebullient manner.

'I am glad you find it so amusing, Mister Holmes!' she said, giving him an acid glance. 'Whoever it was mentioned the name "Henry Gray": something like, "Let me take her to see Henry Gray." I think it was when I was crossing the road earlier – my memory is really so vague here – it's difficult to be more precise.' The woman sighed and dabbed her forehead with Eau de Cologne.

Holmes sprang from his chair and made a grab for his hat. 'I am indebted to you, Your Ladyship! Come, Watson! We have work to do!' said he.

'Catch the villain, Mister Holmes!' she said coldly. 'My nerves are sedated with tincture of opium and a lady of my position is confined to a wheeled chair, else forced to hobble about London on sticks – which is quite intolerable!'

As our cab rattled along Sloane Street with its long line of terraces, the rosy-bricked frontages of the houses for the most part concealed by the dun-coloured fog, conversation could hardly be described as animated.

'Well, we have our cockney, at least!' I remarked.

Holmes had his knees curled up to his chin and was peering out of the window as a child might, watching the passing traffic. His great mind, however, centred upon other things.

'I doubt it,' he said. 'You hardly need to be a remarkable linguist to imitate a cockney accent, Watson!' And he left it at that.

For myself, I reflected, perhaps somewhat morbidly, that public confidence – always a necessary commodity in a profession such as my own – had clearly suffered a considerable blow from the notoriety achieved by this medical fiend!

Our cab left us on the corner of Flood Street and we crossed over the road and followed the

26

same route Lady Stoker-Brant had taken the previous night, taking a leisurely stroll along the Embankment through the fog, which seemed less dense beside the river. I observed the pleasant prospect of Cheyne Walk. Each fashionable villa enjoyed its own agreeable atmosphere of intimacy. The crystal-clear, else diamond-paned windows blazed softly with the gleam of gas-jets. Upon our left-hand side lay the Thames, with Battersea Bridge upstream and the greyish, shadowy aspect of a long frontage of lamp-lit warehouses and quays lined with merchant sailing vessels loading and discharging cargo vaguely visible upon the opposite bank.

At a point just beyond the bridge there was a broader stretch of the river and beached upon the mud flats at low tide a shallow sail barge and a bevy of houseboats.

For some reason, my companion seemed particularly interested in one of these floating dens. He sprang on to the Embankment wall and peered intently at the hull. A thin, smile crept across his lips and he gave a rueful laugh.

'Well, it rhymes, at least!' said he, jumping down again. 'Remain here for the time being, my dear Watson! I shall return presently!'

He ran down a flight of stone steps and trudged across the shimmering mudflats to take a closer look.

I confess the houseboat presented a sorry aspect, for her timbers were covered with a thick, glutinous coat of white paint, with rusty stains near the bows and the heavily tarred seams of her muddy hull were spangled in weed. The cabin, bereft of maritime artistry or design, was adorned with a dull iron funnel: the overall effect upon the aesthetic being one of 'Why on earth is such a thing called either a house or a boat?'

I lit a cigarette and dreamily surveyed the river, watching a steel barque gracefully glide past with her attendant flotilla of barges and lighters.

'The place is deserted – you will observe the name of the vessel?' said Holmes upon his return.

'The *Pendril Gay*,' said I.

'And what can you deduce from that?'

'Perhaps the vessel was christened after some kind of marsh-land bird – you shall have to join a duck shoot, else ask a professional wildfowler!' I replied good-humouredly.

'Has it occurred to you Watson, that the names "Henry Grey" and *Pendril Gay* sound rather alike?'

'They could be loosely described as similar,' I admitted.

'Loosely! My dear Watson,' exclaimed my companion, tapping his cane upon the pavement. 'the names are distinctly alike! Why, a person could easily mistake one for the other!'

Holmes thrust a piece of note-paper into my hand. 'An altogether accurate facsimile – copied by myself from a notice nailed directly above the cabin door.'

I considered the wording carefully:

The PENDRIL GAY: for Sale.
The owner is, at present, abroad in France and does not wish to re-let the above.
All enquiries, Alexander Lovesay & Co.

Solicitor & Commissioner of Oaths,
29, The High Street,
Battersea.
July, 1893.

'But the year is 1895,' said I, somewhat puzzled.
'Evidently there have been no takers, Watson! The vessel receives a coat of paint and tar every twelve months and is duly left to its own rack and ruin – long forgotten by either its owner or his solicitor!'

We trudged along the muddy river bank and boarded the vessel once more.

Whilst I wandered about amidships checking the port-hole windows and skylight for a possible means of entry, my colleague applied his considerable criminal acumen to the problem at hand, and improvised magnificently.

'The lock has recently been changed, Watson,' he said with an almost nonchalant air, digging into his pockets for a pipe knife and inserting the end of this into the lock. He sprang it almost at once and the sliding door was flung back on its castors. We crept down the accommodation ladder and were met below with the smell of soap, with over-tones of paraffin and tobacco.

The cabin was sparsely furnished, with long cushion-covered seats flanking either side. A chimney stove stood at the far end and adjacent to this was a fold-up washstand. A large scrubbed deal table stood in the centre of the cabin with a paraffin lamp hanging above it. The walls were fitted with wooden panels and one of these boards had come loose. The pegs did not fix squarely and without much difficulty I managed to prise it free.

My colleague, who had been poking about amongst the fine, grey ash at the bottom of the stove with his cane, left off what he was doing and came over to join me.

I can honestly say that I shared Holmes's keen sense of anticipation as he reached into the hidden recess but, sometimes a feeling akin to horror will lay hold of you, as it did on this particular occasion when I discovered what lay inside.

Careful not to touch the razor-sharp serrated edge of the blade, Holmes placed the surgical saw under the faint streak of light emitted from the skylight. The letter 'M' was clearly inscribed in gold leaf on the tortoiseshell handle.

I stretched my hand behind the panel to see if there was anything else lurking there and came away with a lidless cardboard box. It contained a surgical knife, smaller knives, large rolls of bandage and some suture needles.

'I believe we have discovered his lair,' said I, with a shudder.

The items were restored to their original home and the loose panel hastily knocked back into place.

With one last look around the cabin we quit the *Pendril Gay*, and I wondered at the deranged psyche of someone capable of employing such impeccable planning to advance his own wicked ends.

'What are we to do now, Holmes?' I enquired.

'Your old medical directory proved invaluable, dear chap, for I took the precaution of compiling a list of the names and addresses of each doctor living in, or with a working practice in, the vicinity of the Embankment. Included are those listed under the letter M: Doctors Minton, Maddon and Mulberry being amongst them!'

'Are we to trek all about Chelsea?' said I, not much liking the prospect.

'It's a long shot I know, Watson, but at least our search shall be narrowed down – somewhat!'

By six o'clock that evening, Holmes and I had visited some ten addresses, including a Doctor Mitchell, M.D., Doctor Joseph Montague (a Doctor of Philosophy as it turned out!), Doctor Percival Maddon M.D. and Doctor Julius Marsh, none of whom seemed likely candidates. I confess that at this juncture I had grown weary of what seemed like an eternal tramp and longed for a good dinner served in the cosy and congenial surroundings of Baker Street.

Our next port of call was a fine Georgian residence with a white stucco frontage, sash windows and black iron railings, situated in Elm Park Road. This belonged to Doctor Theodore Morphius, consultant at 'The London' and, as it turned out, a prospective Member for Parliament.

Holmes rang the bell-pull and not long after the housekeeper, a buxom woman going by the name of Stevens, answered the door.

'Doctor Morphius is, at present, engaged in a debate and not likely to return from the hospital for some time,' she said.

'Do you, by any chance, recall where Doctor Morphius was on the night of Wednesday last, say between the hours of nine and midnight?' asked Holmes.

'That's perfectly simple,' said another voice from within the house. A tall, handsome young gentleman, impeccably dressed in frock coat and spats and smoking an exotically perfumed cigarette came forward and stood beneath the porch lantern for a moment.

I detected a certain air of vanity, or perhaps was it arrogance, about this fellow's character.

He took a puff of his cigarette and leaned against the front entrance porch. 'Doctor Morphius spent the latter part of Wednesday evening working in his study. I believe he also visited the Berkely Club – you are aware of the address, I trust – good night!'

Holmes was just going to leave when there occurred a curious about-turn and he chose to adopt a rather condescending tone to his voice. 'I see you have neglected to clean your boots properly – you are the doctor's valet, I take it?'

Evidently the young man's pride had been delivered a severe blow for he clenched his fists angrily and shouted, 'How dare you address me in those terms, Sir! I will have you know that I am the consultant's son, Jonathan Morphius! Now kindly get off the property or I shall set the dogs on you!'

The interview ended. It had, if nothing else, succeeded in raising my temper considerably.

'I should like to have given that impertinent young fellow a good thrashing!' said I, rummaging in my coat pocket for a cigar as we walked along Elm Park Road.

'Did you happen to observe the brand of cigarette

he smokes, Watson?' asked my colleague as we turned the corner of Church Street.

'I believe it was Turkish – the smell is quite distinctive!'

'Actually it was an Egyptian One Hundred, exclusively purchased from the tobacconist, Lewis's, in Broadway, Westminster – a commendable try though!'

We stood underneath a street lamp and as I lit my cigar, my colleague took the remainder of a half-smoked cigarette from his pocket – recovered earlier from the stove upon the houseboat and exclaimed, 'Now examine this beneath the lamp, Watson – pray, what do you deduce from it?'

'Why, it is the exact same brand,' said I.

'Did you perchance remember something else – a mere nervous habit of his, I suppose – the singular way in which he held the cigarette betwixt finger and thumb and made fine creases along the paper with the sharp end of his thumbnail – why, these are the exact same marks!'

'An astute observation!' I acknowledged.

'I think, perhaps, we should contact Inspector Lestrade – a warrant will be required to search the house.'

'You shall need good grounds for doing so!' I said, clapping my hands together, for it had grown quite cold.

'Oh, I have one, Watson – several of them, in fact!'

And, saying no more upon the matter, we immediately summoned a cab to the nearest telegraph office.

That evening, a little after seven, Inspector Lestrade met us outside Bertrands restaurant in the King's Road. He had managed to obtain the warrant and yet seemed a trifle nervous about implementing the document, for it appeared he had met with a great flourish of weighty objections from every branch of the Scotland Yard tree! Sir Frank Ludlam, the Deputy Commissioner, had reminded his subordinate of the professional status the doctor enjoyed at 'The London' – being also a member of the Medical Council of Great Britain. Other high-ranking colleagues deemed the exercise politically sensitive and not conducive with good promotion prospects either. In layman's terms, Morphius, senior, possessed many friends in high places. However, my esteemed colleague's reputation in the end prevailed.

'The gentleman enjoys considerable fame and is about to enter politics,' said Lestrade.

'Unfortunately, crime – in particular murder – knows no such boundaries of class, else, constituency ambition, Inspector. Do you wish this case to be concluded swiftly?'

'Certainly!'

'Then, to succeed you must carry out my directions as contained in the wire.'

'And you know the identity of the "amorous surgeon", Mister Holmes?'

'I do!'

'And the proof?'

'I am certain lies within that house – so let us waste no more time and go about finding it!'

Together we took a cab to Elm Park Road and

this time were met by the doctor's private secretary, a chap going by the name of Witty.

Lestrade spoke with a strong resolve. 'I am a detective from Scotland Yard and I have a warrant to search this address. Is Doctor Morphius at home, by any chance?'

Lestrade posted a constable outside on the porch and demanded to be taken to see the consultant.

Holmes meanwhile ignored the secretary, Witty, and charged upstairs to the landing. He commandeered a chambermaid and asked to be directed to where the son slept. I followed and we were shown the room.

The private apartment was dominated by a study mantelpiece with all the masculine hallmarks of swords, hunting guns and armour about the fireplace and classical figures from Greek mythology carved in the oaken screen above the mirror. Hangings and fashionable curtains graced the large windows and there were also armchairs and a cabinet therein. A stucco archway led directly into a personal bathroom. While the maid remained outside the door sobbing, and on the verge of hysteria, my colleague examined various artefacts on the mantelpiece and, thereafter, with a good deal of gusto, searched beneath the young gentleman's divan. This proved most opportune for amongst the cricket bats and other sports paraphernalia he discovered a number of leather-bound cases. He chose the largest of these and hurried downstairs.

The atmosphere in the drawing room was very grim indeed. Lestrade, persistent almost to the degree of rudeness, had not allowed anyone to leave and I knew by the acid looks he was giving the consultant that Doctor Morphius, the elder, was in his mind, at least, the prime suspect in the affair.

The consultant examined his gold repeater and thereafter the clock on the mantelpiece chimed the half-hour. Here then was a senior member of my profession, a gentleman of Gladstonian vigour and reserve, already prematurely aged by the cares of high office and about to ascend the slippery ladder of political fame at Westminster.

'What is the meaning of this outrage, Sir?' he finally boomed, losing control of his temper.

The young gentleman stood behind his father, maintaining a calm indifference to the proceedings. He adjusted his wing collar, loosening the stud a little, and then brushed his sleeve lightly with the back of his hand.

'I say it again, Sir! What is the meaning of this confounded outrage?' Morphius slammed his fist down upon the table, knocking over a silver vase and making the port decanter, shiver.

'I will remind you, gentlemen, that I am about to despatch my personal landau to Scotland Yard. My secretary is instructed to fetch the Deputy Commissioner, and you shall hear more of the matter, I think!'

'I apologise for this wretched flight of inconvenience,' Holmes said with a graceful bow. He then took Lestrade to one side and spoke with him.

After this brief and whispered communication, the representative of Scotland Yard turned to face

Morphius, the younger, and said, sternly: 'I must inform you that you are under arrest for the murder of Adelaine Pardoe, lady-in-waiting to the Duchess of Roxborough, and upon another count, concerning a distant cousin of Her Majesty the Queen, Lady Stoker-Brant.'

Morphius the elder, a man of honour and a gentleman, did not hesitate to confront his son directly. 'What have you done?' he said, gravely. 'Tell me you are innocent of these preposterous charges levelled against you!'

The young gentleman was about to speak when my colleague presented him with the leather case he had discovered upstairs.

'Do you know what this is?' said he, speaking to Morphius the elder.

The consultant sighed. 'Yes, I do. It is my old instrument case – one of a set I kept as a young medical student at Barts. A sentimental keepsake, if you like.' He snatched the case from my companion and unfastened the lid. 'This one contains my old surgical saw – such a distinctive tortoise-shell handle – don't you see?'

The case was empty.

'I see your surgical saw has been misplaced, Doctor Morphius, and I think I know where to find it – it will match the indenture perfectly, I am certain!'

'But where on earth did you get this from?' the consultant parried uneasily.

'Beneath your son's divan, along with another interesting item. Here is a silk garter – neatly trimmed around the edges with lace. Peculiarly enough, Lady Stoker-Brant owns a similar article and Adelaine Pardoe was given one by an unknown admirer, shortly before her death!'

Morphius the younger took an Egyptian cigarette from a box upon the mantelpiece and lit it.

'Father,' he said at length, 'perhaps, it is prudent that I should accompany these gentlemen back to Scotland Yard, after all. This matter can be best settled there. Would you be good enough to inform Mister George Lewis that his services may be required?'

'I shall despatch my secretary to Portland Place at once!' came the gruff retort.

'Then – let us, at least, part as friends,' said the young man.

He stretched out his hand but his father refused it and, with his back facing us, Morphius the elder indicated that my colleague should come closer.

'You shall be hearing from my solicitor in the morning, Mister Holmes. My son is wholly innocent of the slightest impropriety!'

'I fear your voice betrays your real feelings upon the matter!'

The old gentleman ignored this, telling comment and answered brusquely, 'I have letters to write – you must excuse me, gentlemen. Please leave my house this instant!'

The trial at the Old Bailey lasted three weeks. Jonathan Morphius, a student of medicine at Cambridge University, was sentenced to be hanged for the murder of Adelaine Pardoe. The dreadful injury inflicted upon the person of Lady Stoker-Brant was also taken into account by the judge.

There is an interesting footnote: we received a request from Mister George Lewis, the solicitor, to visit his client, Jonathan Morphius, upon the morning of the execution, in his cell at Pentonville Prison. Apparently, the young man had something of importance he wished to convey personally to my esteemed colleague. We duly arrived at the appointed hour. The condemned prisoner, like so many before him, seemed not unduly worried about his fate and, despite the close proximity of the gallows shed, appeared calm and industrious.

The old warder, Parker, had just delivered the prisoner's last breakfast – beefsteak, eggs, toast and a tumbler of grog. He took my colleague aside and said, in a low voice, 'The hangman has just arrived to set things to order. Not too long a word if you please, Mister Holmes, the time is nearly upon us, you understand?'

'What is it you wish to tell me?' said Holmes, lighting a cigarette. 'We shall not be overheard.'

Morphius ate a little of his beefsteak and after a pause for reflection had this to say: 'None of the street-women suspected of course – I never did get buckled – you see, I was but an innocent, cherub-faced youth at the time.'

My colleague leaned forward and listened the more intently.

'I thought what a genius I should be.' He dabbed his chin with a napkin and smiled. 'If, at the precocious age of thirteen years I could but master certain aspects of female anatomy. By this time, my father was already a much regarded consultant, idolised by his students at The London. I felt certain he should be much impressed if I could but further my own knowledge on the subject and to this end earn a little of the respect I deserved, as his only son and heir.'

'And, what of the women involved?' said Holmes.

'Those common harlots!' He scowled. 'Mere drunken trollops who since my dear mother's death I knew Father regularly consorted with at such low places as The Eagle in City Road, Whitechapel, else, the Haymarket. They were to be offered up for dissection to that great God science. Their destiny was to be intertwined with my own – irrevocably so. Annie Chapman, for instance. I adored her pluck yet even her indomitable spirit, her determination not to become the victim deserted her at the last. Mary Jane Kelly, the lady with whom my father seemed particularly enamoured – I spent a little more time with her at Miller Court, but, I fear the prison chaplain and the hangman approaches – how perfectly tiresome!'

He sighed and took a sip of whisky.

'I should have liked very much to dictate my memoirs for posterity. The "ginny kidney" and accompanying note sent to Mister Lusk was, of course, but a prank any medical student should have been proud of, but nothing to do with me! I sometimes threw away my knives at Smithfield meat market – where they should not look at all conspicuous!'

'And you purportedly ceased your activities after the fifth victim?' my colleague asked.

'The figure you give is inaccurate but I shall not trifle with mere conundrums. I was sent to Eton and thence to Cambridge, Mister Holmes, and yet I have still managed to indulge my fancy from time to time.'

He put aside his plate and even at this dreadful hour did not betray the slightest melancholy or repentant emotion whatsoever; indeed, he seemed to revel in the memory of his past sins. He smiled thinly. 'But, our brief interview must come to a close, I fear!'

And so we hastened away from that dreadful place.

However, at this juncture, I propose to let the discerning reader of this chronicle judge the character of this madman's confession for themselves. The insane ramblings of an egotist? Well, despite the endless and tiresome conjecture surrounding the identity of 'Jacky the Terror' as he was commonly known amongst those unfortunate enough to live within the derelict precincts of Whitechapel, I think it certainly offers, for the first time, a plausible alternative.

3

The Missing Earl

'The Earl of Donerly is missing,' said I, over the breakfast table one morning, as Holmes attacked his second egg.

'I'm absolutely ravenous, Watson! I spent all last night in the mortuary at Clerkenwell studying a cadaver!'

'Did you have an interesting specimen to work with?'

I knew my friend was keenly interested in every aspect of criminal investigation and imagined the police were puzzled over some unnatural, else, unexplained death.

'Drowned in the Thames, Watson,' said Holmes.

'I'm surprised,' said I. 'The River Authority rarely keep the bodies at Clerkenwell.'

'Referring to your earlier point, Watson, the corpse in question was that of an elderly woman from the East End of London, last seen alive by a costermonger selling matches off Honduras Wharf, near Saint Paul's, to a foreign sailor. All the forensic evidence suggests sudden death by drowning, although how her body ended up closeted in the basement of a public house in Kennington, wrapped in newspaper, must for the time being remain a singularly perplexing mystery. Did you mention the Earl of Donerly, by the way?'

'Yes, the *Telegraph* and *The Times* both mention his mysterious disappearance at the funeral.'

'At the funeral? Whose funeral?'

'Sir Walter Wallington, the Earl's uncle apparently.'

'That's the famous archaeologist, Wallington, isn't it?'

'Yes.'

I handed the newspaper to Holmes and let him read the article, while I left the table and went over to my armchair.

It was a bitterly cold morning and there had been a frost overnight. The window panes were tinged with a thick covering of ice crystals. I regarded the smouldering fire – barely alight in the grate – and, with a firm resolve, decided to attack it with the poker and liven it up a bit. Just as the flames started to leap about, I heard the doorbell clang downstairs and a short while later a gentleman wearing a black top hat and sombre frock coat entered the room. He held a copy of *The Times* under his arm.

'Good-day, gentlemen. I trust I did not interrupt your breakfast?'

'Breakfast is finished!' said Holmes, looking up from the paper. 'Do you require coffee – if so, there is still plenty in the pot.'

'Thank you, that should be most agreeable,' the man said, taking off his hat.

'Did you take the Metropolitan?' said I, refilling my pipe.

'No, I took a cab,' he replied.

'Hum – you have come about the Donerly affair, I take it?' said Holmes. 'I perceive you are wearing a black armband. Here, take this cup and come over by the fire, you look frozen!'

'And you, Sir, I take it, must be Mister Sherlock Holmes?'

My companion nodded. 'And, this is my colleague, Doctor Watson. Do you smoke? Here, have a cigar. How was the traffic this morning by the way? Slow, I should imagine.'

'Dreadfully slow, Mister Holmes.'

'Have you come far?'

'From Hampstead – though I live and work in Edinburgh.'

'Ah, the young Earl is, of course, Scottish?'

'Yes, my name is Timpson and I am the family solicitor. I accompanied the Earl down to London for the funeral.'

'Don't they have a castle in Leith?'

'Yes, his mother, Lady McGregor, stays there. She is an invalid and gave up her town house in Chelsea some years ago. Her ladyship was first informed of Wally's illness three weeks ago but, when it became apparent that the poor old thing was sinking fast, she asked Charlie to go in her place and represent the clan. However, she thought it prudent that I should accompany the young Earl down to London and keep an eye on him. He is extremely fond of the turf and was intimate with certain stables and gallops at Epsom.'

'He owns a race-horse, then?'

'He used to own a score of them – although the

45

Earl possesses little business acumen, he loves a race or the sales ring. That said, it is necessary to back a winner once in a while. His best jockey unfortunately resigned last year and despite investing a fortune in bloodstock, none of his horses ever made the running. Furthermore, the reliance he continually placed upon others for advice led to embarrassing pecuniary circumstances!'

'In short, he was in debt!'

'Exactly, Mister Holmes. The poignant anxiety of his mother was pathetic to behold. You must realise that her late husband's high position as Commander in Chief Elect of the Fifth Highland Fusiliers, along with his exemplary military and political record, made the situation highly delicate and I was, at length, summoned to Leith Castle and informed of certain difficulties that had arisen.

'A Greek gentleman by the name of Count Alberto Venizilos claimed that the young Earl had purchased from him a colt named Saracen Diamonds, and that, although the horse had come in a poor tenth at Newmarket and consequently fallen and broken its neck at Aintree, the money in lieu of several months' good grace had not been forthcoming!'

'And how much was the nag really worth?' said I.

'With hindsight, Doctor Watson, its real value is not hard to determine,' said Timpson, with a cynical glance at my companion. 'However, the Count produced certain certificates – every one purportedly signed and counter-signed, to the tune of fifty thousand guineas, by the young Earl himself. The Earl of Donerly denied he ever purchased the horse and claimed the signatures were a forgery. Count Venizilos threatened a law suit and, in doing so, played his best card. The matter was now perilously close to entering the public domain and a compromise had to be found quickly.

'At Lady McGregor's request, I consulted the eminent barrister, Sir Humphrey Arden, Q.C., an expert in criminal libel and renowned for obtaining exemplary damages for his clients. After weighing the facts, he advised me that the money must be somehow found and the matter settled out of court.

'I knew, of course, that neither he nor his clerk would have accepted such a brief. Apart from the close friendship he enjoyed with Lady McGregor's late husband and the high esteem in which he always held that venerable Scotsman – hero of Tel-El-Kebir and Osmansi – Sir Humphrey was acquainted with Lady McGregor's personal physician and must have known of her fragile health and realised her weak constitution should never have survived the strain of open court and the ensuing publicity. On my instructions, she agreed to pay the Count the fifty thousand guineas.'

'The Earl is normally an affectionate and considerate man?' said Holmes.

'Certainly!'

'I imagine these advisers took advantage of him – perhaps they were part of some criminal cartel?'

'More to the point Mister Holmes, Count Alberto Venizilos, the "mystery man of Europe", may be back in London!'

'To extort some more money from the young Earl by means of blackmail?' said I.

'Indeed! He has apartments in the Hotel d'Angleterre at Patras near Olympia and also Monte Carlo. An avid follower of the sport of kings, he could have come here to attend the Ponsonby Handicap at Newmarket.'

'Then we must act quickly. I shall telegraph the Foreign Office at once! There is a Greek delegation presently staying at the Carlton Hotel, they might be able to help trace Count Venizilos. Meanwhile, I should like to pay a visit to Sir Walter Wallington's house in Hampstead, Mister Timpson.'

After certain messages had been left with Mrs Hudson to despatch, post-haste, to the telegraph office, the four-wheeler – with its bell tinkling furiously – rattled off down Baker Street and we arrived in Hampstead village at about ten o'clock. There, we ascended a steep rise. The air was crisp and invigorating, the sky was slightly overcast in anticipation of rain. At the brow of the hill, the cabby whipped his horses and we trotted down a cul-de-sac to a tiny hamlet of houses backing on to the wooded heath.

Timpson possessed a key and we let ourselves into the place. The rooms were deserted and, in many cases, the furniture covered in dust-sheets. Over every mirror hung dreary funerary drapes of black bombazine.

We went straightaway to Sir Walter's study.

Holmes flung back the curtains and let some light penetrate the stilted atmosphere. There upon the desk, just as the great man had left them, were his pipes and other personal effects. The shelves were filled with countless souvenirs and mementos from his various expeditions and digs and, on the walls were photographs of Wallington in Egypt, Wallington in Nova Scotia and Wallington up the Zambezi River.

Above the marble fireplace, hung upon two large brass hooks, was a shovel. The inscription beneath this queer trophy read: 'With this spade I first struck the Tomb of Atara. Wallington.'

Whilst Holmes studied the spade with some interest – 'A fine specimen of a shovel, Watson, though I fear a little battered by time and not much use in the garden!' – I went over to the large dormer window and lit a cigarette. At the end of the garden I saw what I, at first, supposed to be a simple dovecot, surrounded by a clump of trees.

'The mausoleum,' Timpson said, drawing the curtain back a little further. 'Wallington had it erected for himself and his wife, Catherine. Alas, she departed this world a while back and he now lies alongside her.'

Upon the domed roof of the tomb I observed a marble statuette of the Egyptian Queen Nefertari.

'A most impressive structure,' commented Holmes, who had joined us. 'But, pray, what have we next door?'

We passed into another room and Timpson explained: 'The "lying-in-state" room, Mister Holmes. Many of us came in here to pay our last respects to Wally – toast him in champagne, if you like!'

'And when was this?'

'Upon the eve of the funeral after a wake supper.'

Here was a spacious apartment – panelled high up its walls, more than thirty feet long, and lit by a great mullioned bay window which gazed on to the lawn. The marble fireplace, surmounted by a Grecian over-mantle, was dominated by an early photograph of the archaeologist, wreathed in black binding. There was little furniture save the bier, intended to support the coffin.

'Wallington was evidently a tall fellow, Mister Timpson, for the bier supports have been placed a considerable distance apart.'

'That is so, Mister Holmes. He was well over six feet tall and stocky to boot. Eight bearers carried the coffin to the mausoleum, for it was so heavy.'

Holmes went over to the bier and examined the floor-boards directly beneath with his magnifying lens.

'Preposterous!' he yelled. 'Throw back the velvets, Watson, and let some more light in!'

I did as my friend requested and we watched with considerable interest as Holmes, with his nose to the ground, studied the floor-boards once more. He sprang to his feet and chose not to slow the pace of his investigation by offering us any explanation for his sudden outburst. Instead, he pointed towards the door.

'Now, I should very much like to visit the Earl's bedroom. Would you be so kind as to lead the way, Mister Timpson?'

Upstairs we visited the guest bedroom. As opposed to the drabness of the mourning chamber, this room was light and airy. The Earl's baggage was heaped in the corner and perched upon the top of a cupboard. There was a divan and a tiny cabinet with a glass of water and a travelling clock ticking frantically away upon it.

'Nothing has been disturbed, I take it?' asked my companion.

'Everything in the room is exactly as I found it, Mister Holmes, upon the morning of the Earl's disappearance.'

'You will observe the alarm of the travelling clock is set for two in the morning Watson! A little early, don't you think, considering Sir Walter's funeral was not until half-past nine? Incidentally, did the young Earl ever wear slippers while he stayed here, Mister Timpson?'

'Yes, he did, Mister Holmes. I remember he wore a pair of Turkish slippers about the house. He was rather fond of them.'

'Now, perhaps, we should go downstairs and visit the garden?'

We went outside and I stood under a trellis walk covered with creeper and imagined nothing could be more charming in spring or summer – the long beds of flowering shrubs, the greenhouse glittering in the sunlight, the high boundary wall with its clay bricks well seasoned by weather, and the picturesque old sun-dial in the middle of the lawn, stained with lichen. And, yet, at this time of year the garden had a rather melancholy look about it.

We ambled down to the greenhouse and behind were neatly laid-out flower beds and a fair-sized vegetable garden. This interested Holmes and he stood and meditated upon it for a while. There was a light scattering of leaves covering the top soil and, at least twenty bamboo canes with labels attached.

'Could you tell me what it says on that label, the third one along, Watson?'

'Really, Holmes!' I ejaculated. 'Can you not read it for yourself? The inscription says plainly "winter cabbage"!'

'A row of winter cabbage!' answered Holmes, with considerable amusement. 'And, pray, what type of vegetable is planted along that row?'

'Onions!' said I. 'The gardener has mixed up the labels. He is evidently a sloppy fellow!'

Timpson disagreed. 'Nonsense! Alfred is on the contrary a most meticulous fellow. He was head gardener on Lady McGregor's estate for twenty years and she would never hire an incompetent – let alone recommend him to Sir Walter!'

'Ha!' said Holmes, gaily taking my arm and hurrying away. 'You know, Watson,' he whispered, 'I've never really been that keen on gardening, have you?'

We continued down the path and came to a wicket gate. The Wallington tomb stood behind a clump of trees, wreathed in mist. Queen Nefertari stared down at us with white, pupil-less eyes.

Quite unexpectedly, Holmes went up to the tomb and struck it hard with his stick and, thereafter, walked around it a couple of times, tapping the stonework at intervals.

'You will observe there is no entrance to the mausoleum, Watson. Pray, how exactly was the tomb sealed, Mister Timpson?'

'The coffin was placed inside and the internment door secured by the undertaker. The workmen then bricked it up and covered the stone-work with plaster.'

'And who holds the key?'

'There was only one ever cast. Directly after the funeral the undertaker had it melted down into a memoriam coin and despatched to Lady McGregor's castle in Scotland.'

'Well, it certainly seems impregnable from the resurrection men,' said I.

No sooner had we got back to the house than the doorbell rang. Timpson went to answer it and the caller was none other than Inspector Lestrade of Scotland Yard. He took off his hat and came in.

'The foreigner?' he said, taking out his address book.

'Count Venizilos,' said I.

'Yes, the Greek gentleman – I have a score of detectives and constables in plain clothes mingling with the racing fraternity at Newmarket. No doubt the young Earl is amongst their number suitably disguised and the scoundrel is anxious to meet him!'

'I hear the running is good to fair, although they are expecting some rain this afternoon, apparently,' said Holmes, leaning against the banister and smoking his pipe.

'I am confident we shall have this fellow, Venizilos, and the young Earl, safely under custody by this evening,' continued Lestrade.

'Yes, and I suppose Arthur Holt's Green Damson shall win the Ponsonby Handicap, a rank outsider, of course!' snorted Holmes.

'I should not put a penny on that old nag. The trainer resigned and, why, Green Damson has not won a race all season!'

'And, Inspector,' said Holmes, sarcastically, 'I should not put a penny on your finding the Earl of Donerly at Newmarket, either!'

Lestrade looked extremely puzzled. 'And, why do you say that, Mister Holmes? You evidently know something about this case that I do not!'

'You shall not find the Earl at Newmarket, for the simple reason he has not travelled up there! However, if you would be good enough to join me tonight, say, at one, I shall endeavour to locate him for you!'

We left Timpson in good spirits, took a cab and returned to our diggings in Baker Street. By the time we reached Marylebone it was dark and raining heavily. The darting umbrellas of the pedestrians and the hazy gleam of gas lamps reflected upon the glassy surface of the pavements.

Mrs Hudson had earlier prepared dinner and we ate this – for the most part – in silence. After our meal, I sat in my armchair smoking a cigar and watched Holmes take down his clay pipe from the mantelpiece. As he recharged his pipe with the strongest black tobacco, I detected a somewhat quizzical look in his eye.

'Hum, have you the time, Watson?' said he, stretching out his long legs in front of the hearth.

'A quarter past eight,' said I, glancing at my pocket watch.

'What do you know of Sir Walter Wallington?'

'I should say from our earlier visit to his house that his career was an industrious one, although I confess I have not followed it very closely.'

'Quite so! Do you recall the shovel hanging about the mantelpiece in his study?'

'Yes I do. Some queer inscription about the Tomb of Atara!'

'That particular expedition was the last trip he ever made to Egypt.'

'Oh, had he no more mummies to dig up in the desert then?' said I.

'The Egyptian authorities would not allow him back in, Watson!'

'And, why is that?' I asked.

'I have a newspaper cutting here that I think you will find interesting. I read this article in *The Times* some years back and buried it away in my scrapbook for posterity. It is a trifle yellow with age, but nonetheless perfectly readable.'

I took the scrap of paper and held it under the lamp. It read thus:

Egyptians doubt Sir Walter's word
Grave ornaments missing. Sacred Tomb
of Princess Atara defiled.

Sudanese archaeologist Edal Grafium, the present proprietor of the Khartoum Museum of Natural History, sides with Egyptian government and claims to have found no evidence, whatsoever, to suggest that the tomb had been desecrated six centuries earlier by grave bandits as Sir Walter inferred. Indeed, he apparently had good cause to believe Sir Walter, himself, had stolen the gold and run it across the desert to Begum, a port on the west coast of Africa and thence by steamer to Europe. The Foreign Office, however, were quick to dismiss the allegations as scurrilous and unfounded. Sir Walter, himself, said they were laughable. 'The only thing I got out of that tomb was an old mummy, a bad back and a good deal of dust,' he told reporters.

'It does seem rather odd that a common shovel should be raised above the mantelpiece as a trophy. If the actual find was so trivial, why go to such lengths to commemorate it, and if he did, indeed, snatch the grave ornaments, what actually became of them? Has the British Museum acquired the treasures, or did he manage to sell to some enterprising collector?'

'I think it highly probable, Watson, that the Atara treasure remained in Sir Walter's possession.'

'He did not sell for financial reasons then?'

'I doubt it! At the time of the expedition to Egypt he was already a wealthy man, although, I grant you, the treasure was priceless.'

'He preferred to gloat over it, then?' said I.

'Quite possibly, Watson,' replied my companion, not wishing to give anything else away.

Later that night, we took a cab back to Hampstead and accompanied by Inspector Lestrade went into the garden and made our way down the path, using our umbrellas to fend off the ferocious wind and rain. When we reached the wicket gate, one of our dark lanterns blew out and the other flickered woefully, close to extinction.

'Strike a match somebody!' said Timpson, shaking the lantern and attempting to dampen the wick.

'Is that what you have dragged us out here to

look at, Mister Holmes?' said Lestrade, striking at his tinder box to little effect.

I observed the clump of trees blowing about in the gale. Nefertari stood upon the great domed roof of the tomb, with water cascading down her marble robes in torrents.

Lestrade could not hide his frustration. 'Did you really expect to encounter the Earl down here in this weather, Mister Holmes? Is he, at present, taking a leisurely stroll across Hampstead Heath, I wonder?'

'I suppose you could say it is an encounter of sorts, although I fear we may have some time to wait, Lestrade. I think these bushes over here should provide adequate cover.'

So we waited and in that time the rain never ceased for more than ten minutes. I knelt under my dripping umbrella, experiencing a comfortless nether-doze – a shadowy purgatory where I dreamt of my bed and the dim imaginings of a fire ...

Holmes suddenly shook me by the arm.

'Watson, wake up! Listen, can you hear?'

I confess I could hear nothing apart from the rain, and then...

Tap, tap, silence. *Tap, tap, clang! Tap, tap*, silence. *Tap, tap, clang!*

'Why, someone is in there!' said I.

'Or, perhaps it is Sir Walter's ghost!' remarked Timpson, by way of a tired attempt at making light of the situation.

The blows quickened! *Clang! Clang! Clang-clank!*

'That's no ghost,' said Lestrade.

We heard some masonry collapse on to the floor

of the tomb and then a loud voice shouted excitedly: 'Eureka!'

After this, silence reigned once more and as time went by no other sound escaped from the tomb and our initial excitement gave way to a general apathy. Then there was an enormous *bang!*

The explosion was a fairly prodigious one! I saw Queen Nefertari, accompanied by a cloud of dust, rise into the air, turn several cartwheels and come crashing down. The marble statue came to rest in the wet grass, broken into three separate pieces.

As the smoke dispersed, a young man covered in dust scrambled out of the ruin, dragging a canvas sack behind him.

'The Earl of Donerly, I believe?' said Holmes, rushing to greet him. 'I trust the bag is not too heavy? Shall I give you a helping hand down with it?'

'I can manage perfectly well, thank you,' said he, jumping from the tomb. 'Oh, there are more of you, are there? Quite a welcome party, I fear!'

The Earl's white hair was matted and his eyes shone all the more vividly for his ghostly visage.

'I trust the accommodation was to your liking, Sir?' said Lestrade, dusting down his coat.

'A little chilly,' the young Earl replied. 'Are, perchance, any of you gentlemen in favour of a glass of something strong – for it is so dreadfully wet out here. I think, perhaps, we should adjourn to Wally's house!'

'And I think there's a great deal of explaining to do!' added Lestrade, seizing the sack of clanking metal objects from the youth and slinging it over his shoulder.

'Was it the noise that alerted you? God knows, I hammered away with a rag but it was so dreadfully slow that, in the end, I abandoned caution to the wind and let fly!'

'I think I first caught a glimpse of your scheme when I discovered particles of gunpowder and metal filings scattered underneath the bier,' remarked Holmes.

'That's smart, Sir! You are the police, I take it?'

My colleague smiled. 'We are roughly half and half. All of us interested parties of course. My name is Sherlock Holmes and this is my colleague, Doctor Watson. May I introduce Inspector Lestrade, who represents Scotland Yard in this affair.'

'Ah, and that's Timpson, of course. I didn't recognise you under all that dust, Sir. Well, it looks as though my ambitions are well and truly scuppered, gentlemen.'

Once we were back at the house the Earl, who, wherever he sat left a dusty mark upon the furniture, handed us each a glass of whisky and soda and we, thereafter, stood to offer him a toast.

'I am sure your dear mother in Scotland shall be greatly relieved that you are in good health and were not at Newmarket for the Ponsonby Handicap,' said Timpson, raising his glass fondly.

'Indeed, Sir, I have not attended a race meeting for some time, although I don't think I shall be taking up this sort of thing for sport either, and I must say, had not the prize been so great, I should never have dared contemplate such a venture.'

'Then, perhaps, I should explain exactly how you

went about it,' said Holmes, lighting his pipe and blowing out a reeking cloud of tobacco smoke.

'I should be all ears, Sir.' The young Earl brushed some more dust from his frock-coat and sat down to listen.

'To begin with, your uncle was a sick man and as he lay dying you stood beside the bed. He was, by this time, delirious and his mind wandering to and fro along the tracks of his long life. His incoherent rambling was, for the most part, like an indecipherable code. Occasionally he would string a complete sentence or two together and you could make out the word "Atara". He kept repeating this over and over again and before he died your uncle quite unconsciously gave away the secret of the missing treasure, stolen many years previously from a tomb in Egypt. He not only revealed what that treasure was but also the place where he had hidden it.'

'Grief, Sir, you are a phantom!' exclaimed the Earl. 'I believe you were beside me at his death-bed, or else, hovered mysteriously above!'

'To continue. It was clear in your own mind that the treasure now lay within your grasp. The tomb was, of course, kept locked and the undertaker had the only key, therefore it was impossible to break in. So you had to hatch a plan. At exactly two o'clock upon the morning of your uncle's funeral, the alarm on your travelling clock went off as planned. You got out of bed, dressed, and then gathering together your bundle of tools along with some other useful accessories, you crept downstairs and visited the lying-in-state room. A coffin can be a most hospitable traveller. A person can lie undetected within its confines and, after having filed down the thread of each screw would be able to elevate the lid at the slightest angle and lower it again whenever necessary with the ends of his fingers, and thereby solve the problem of fresh air, but more importantly, escape!

'A *large* coffin offers endless possibilities, for the occupant can take along a couple of blankets, a paraffin stove, some explosives and provisions with him. But, who was actually inside Sir Walter's coffin on the morning of the funeral, and if he was not there, where was the body?'

My companion re-lit his pipe and walked over to the dormer window.

'I do not profess to be a keen horticulturist, indeed, my interest in gardening is precisely nil and, yet, I can at least recognise the difference between winter cabbage and a row of onions. Earlier it struck me that the vegetable garden had certain irregularities pertaining to it. For instance, the top soil was considerably displaced, and the vegetables had been dug up and replanted. Also, certain of the labels on the bamboo sticks were in the wrong place – for instance, according to one label a row that should have been winter cabbage was, in fact, onions! A row of carrots, turnips and so forth. I was left in no doubt that beneath the vegetable garden there lay a shallow grave in which the remains of Walter Wallington had been interred. Perhaps you could relate the rest of your charnel exploits as they occurred?'

'I should be glad to, Mister Holmes, but everything

you have stated is, in fact, the truth and I take my hat off to you, Sir. My uncle's coffin had been placed near to the stone sarcophagus. I got out and with the paraffin stove barely alight, set about my work, until exhausted and weary of the eternal clang of the hammer echoing around the mausoleum like a tolling bell. I extinguished every flame and collapsed on to the floor where I instantly fell asleep.

'I was next awoken by a loud tapping on the outside of the tomb. I heard voices and feared I may have been discovered but, after a while, the noise ceased altogether and I wearily relit my stove and started work again. The going was hard, for more and more marble was chipped away and, yet, the lid to this wretched sarcophagus was so thick that it took me hours to gain but the slightest headway. In the end, however, I became so impatient that I violently struck away at the stone. The blows rang out until, at last, one mighty blow set the rest to rubble and the lid of the sarcophagus collapsed inwards. There, within its musty confines, I observed my aunt's skull – the sunken sockets staring back at me like grinning black wells. I frantically cleared away the debris and for the first time was able to gaze upon the gorgeous helmet that had once adorned the head of Princess Atara. This and more I snatched from that dusty heap of bones. I retrieved several gold bracelets littered with precious stones and also a priceless girdle. Oh, how the gem stones sparkled – even in that weak glimmer cast by the stove, Mister Holmes!'

'So you had discovered the missing treasure stolen

by your uncle from an Egyptian tomb and presented as a gift to your aunt, Catherine Wallington. A token of his undying affection for her, no doubt! Here, Watson, take a look at this! I found it upon Sir Walter's desk in his study, earlier.'

Holmes took a photograph from his pocket. It had been taken at the Lyceum in the Strand. It was a New Year's fancy dress gala. All the guests had glasses raised and were preparing to toast the actor, Henry Irving. Sir Walter and his wife stood beside Ellen Terry, facing the camera.

'Your aunt was a very handsome woman,' said I, passing the photograph to Lestrade.

'And a very pretty costume she's wearing, I might add, eh, Holmes!' said he. 'None of the guests could have possibly realised that the gold helmet, bracelets and girdle were not mere paste replicas but, the genuine article.'

'Priceless beyond belief!' my friend added. 'Well, Inspector, I am sure Lady McGregor will be delighted her son is safe. I think the Egyptian consul should be alerted at once. No doubt they will compensate the Earl handsomely for the return of the Atara Treasure but I think it would be wise to firstly dig up the vegetable patch and replace Sir Walter safely back in his coffin, before the gardener realises something is amiss! I am certain the hole in the roof of the tomb will not look too queer – these things tend to crumble in time, anyhow – pity about the statue though!'

4

The 'Ring of Stones'

It was a dreary December evening and whilst rain driven by the blustering gale howling about the portals of Baker Street lashed against the window pane, Holmes was busy at his chemistry, conducting some experiment with a beaker of spirit of potassium, one side of his face lit up like a fierce Samurai mask.

I sat down in my armchair and lit a cigar – a committed idler with nothing much to do. I was, therefore, resigned to read a tatty yellow-back novel in which I had not the slightest interest. I had barely consulted the first chapter when he snapped:

'Column four, page eight of the *Telegraph*! There is an article of considerable merit – perhaps, you have overlooked it, Watson?'

I tossed the novel aside and took up the paper instead. A meticulous study of the page eventually gleaned dividends, although barely had I a chance to browse over the article, which concerned the plight of a young girl whom the police believed had been abducted from a Wiltshire village, when the doorbell clanged downstairs and Holmes sprang from his chair and went over to the window.

'The fellow is evidently over-modest, else, extremely self-conscious about his appearance, Watson,' he remarked, standing back a little. 'He wears his best Sunday clothes – even upon a weekday – and possesses the fresh, ruddy complexion and stalwart frame of a farmer or a country gentleman.'

'Well,' I answered, listening to the rain outside. 'I believe Mrs Hudson has just let him in.'

Holmes received our guest warily. He was over six feet tall, broad, ruddy-faced and had an almost apologetic manner.

'My name is Ragthorne, Sir.'

'Well, that's a strange coincidence,' said I, 'for the name Ragthorne is, at present, staring back at me from this page.'

'Halloa! Clara Ragthorne, the missing girl. You are a relation, I take it?' said Holmes, taking our guest's wet things and hanging them up.

'Her grandfather, Sir.'

'I see. Well this is my colleague, Doctor Watson. Pray, take a seat. I should be most interested to listen to what you have to say about the affair. The *Telegraph* is hardly forthcoming but then these rural matters tend to be neglected by the London papers as a rule.'

I sat back, puffing my cigar whilst the old gentleman contemplated the flickering red coals in the hearth, his brow furrowed and his whole aspect deeply melancholy.

'I have a farm on the outskirts of the village of Lower Stowborough in Wiltshire,' he said at length. 'Before I took it over, the land was neglected and the buildings in a poor state of repair. The hardship of inclement weather, misfortune in purchase of stock and several unforeseen legal matters were dealt with easily enough, however, fifteen years ago my daughter-in-law, Anne, died in childbed – a bleak night for us all, Mister Holmes. That damn wind howling about the eaves of the cottage whilst a dead mother lay coffined and her tiny newborn babe wailed like a banshee in the adjoining room. My son was distraught and had not my wife somehow managed to pacify his feelings, well, Edward should have blown his brains out there and then! Thank God, this never came to pass and that tiny babe, christened Clara Dawn, blossomed into one of the prettiest creatures I ever saw. The very image of her mother and blessed with all those same noble qualities.

'So, at the end of last week, as was customary, we visited my son's cottage, The Leas, fully expecting to find our dear grandchild busy about the settle preparing the supper, her happy countenance gracing the parlour as usual. However, the place was entirely deserted – the stove had not even been lit!'

The piteous expression upon the farmer's weather-beaten face intensified as with a watery glimmer in his eye he shook his head and said solemnly: 'Edward returned from the ploughing he had been superintending and observing our anxious faces demanded to know what was the matter.

' "Where is Clara?" he asked.

' "I know not," said I. "Did you, perhaps, send her on some errand?"

' "No, I did not – I have never known her to be

away from the cottage at this late hour! Why, darkness fell a long while ago and the table has not even been laid for supper!"

'And so we stormed out of the cottage and started to search the lanes, but to no avail. None of us have seen nor received any correspondence from Clara since. But this said, I have a young farm apprentice by the name of Carker, who vanished at about the same time. He lived in the agricultural cottages nearby The Leas and I have it on good authority that he stole several pounds from a woman in the village, a poor cripple without legs as it so happens.'

'Are the two disappearances linked in any way, I wonder?' said I.

'Why, Carker is an ugly brute, built like an ox, Doctor Watson! I cannot possibly conceive of my granddaughter eloping with such a person!'

'But the police think differently,' said Holmes.

'Indeed, and this is what rankles, Sir, for they suspect Carker is the culprit and, yet, somehow in my heart I cannot accept this. For all his faults, and there are many of them, I do not believe this lumbering fellow would harm anybody, let alone my granddaughter. He is what could be best described as a gentle giant!'

Holmes fastidiously plucked his oily, black clay from the rack upon the mantelpiece and stood with one hand in the pocket of his dressing gown, over by the bow window. I could observe the reflection of his wan, hawk-like features in the glass.

'And, pray, at what stage did you inform the police, Mister Ragthorne?'

'By the time it had struck eight of the clock and there was still no sign of Clara – Edward and my stockman, Jarvis, went out and searched the lanes once more. I on the other hand ordered my wife to remain behind and await Clara's possible return, and rode in my trap like a damn devil through driving rain, mud and gale until I reached Amesbury, where I searched the town for a constable. Well, Mister Holmes, the matter remains unresolved! I know you are a consulting detective though, God knows, I should never be able to afford your services but, at least, I beg your opinion on the matter. I have commuted down from Salisbury for that very same purpose.'

'You have endured a long train journey all the way from Wiltshire merely to obtain a professional opinion, Mister Ragthorne?'

'I ask no more, Sir! I realise you are a busy man with many clients. Your services are much in demand, but, if there is some hope, however vague, that Clara may yet still be alive then my journey has not been an entirely wasted one.'

'My dear, Sir!' Holmes said, brightly, filling his pipe with tobacco. 'The night is foul – I suggest you share a dinner of wild duck, prepared by our esteemed housekeeper, Mrs Hudson, and take the couch for the night. This case is a singular one and both Doctor Watson and myself shall accompany you back to Wiltshire, tomorrow morning.'

After breakfast the next day, we summoned a cab and arrived at Paddington in good time to catch the train to the West Country. We reached the city of Salisbury, with its magnificent cathedral spire, by mid-afternoon and made the journey down to the village of Lower Stowborough in a four-wheeler. Upon the way we encountered remote, snug hamlets encompassed on every side by plain scenery: the broad Wiltshire acres with their wealth of hedgerow trees, pastures and cultivation, steeped in pre-history.

The Leas was a picturesque cottage with its roof of thatch and rough stone walls coloured with age. Behind it, approached by a winding track, stood the farmhouse backed by a range of old reed-thatched barns and cowsheds. There was a hoar frost and the air had a sharp tang about it. Holmes, nattily dressed in his tweed suit and deer-stalker, sprang down from the four-wheeler and loosely flinging his scarf across his shoulder said, matter-of-factly: 'Watson, would you care to accompany me on a short ramble? The trees at this time of year are so melancholy and the scenery hereabouts is really quite splendid to behold. There is a church I should very much like to visit. I observed the tower earlier from the brow of the hill.'

'That is the church of Saint Magnus in the parish of Upper Wexham, Mister Holmes,' said the old gentleman, unharnessing the horses and about to lead them away to the stock yard.

We had just begun our trek, my attention being wholly preoccupied by the wide open fields and some crows perched upon a wire, when Holmes suddenly bent down and rummaged amongst a clump of grass with his cane. There was something glinting in the winter sunshine and he picked it up.

'Capital, Watson – a bronze medallion, quite an old one by the look of it!'

'Who is this fellow, "William Sturkey", commemorated here?' said I, studying the face on the coin and handing it back to my colleague.

'I haven't the faintest. Probably some philosopher or other?' Holmes remarked, tossing the coin up into the air and catching it again. 'Halloa! The reverse holds certain singular possibilities though. Mister Ragthorne, from Lower Stowborough to Amesbury is a half-mile or so. The eminent archaeologist and numismatist, Professor Andrew Kempe, resides at Brabbenhall Manor on the outskirts of the town: could you look him up for me?'

'I should be delighted! I confess the name means little to me although I have ridden past his house many times.'

'Tell the professor a Mister Sherlock Holmes would like to see him. He once read a lengthy monograph of mine concerning the Buddhism of Ceylon – so he knows of my reputation at least!'

'I shall ride over to Amesbury this minute, Sir,' he replied, leaving one of the horses with a boy.

Holmes placed the coin in his pocket and we resumed our walk. On our left, cut between some banked-up hedgerow trees, I observed a narrow footpath concealed for the most part by thick undergrowth. It led through a wooded dell and culminated at an old, frost-spangled timber stile.

We followed this route and were about to clamber over the rickety structure when Holmes bent down and examined the cross-beam with his magnifying lens. Caught upon a rusty nail was a ragged piece of black cloth not unlike the hem of some garment. My colleague seized this and put it in his pocket.

On the other side of a hill, some way down was a hamlet of agricultural cottages and the ancient church of Saint Magnus, its square Saxon tower overlooking the tiny settlement like some grim sentinel. It appeared every inhabitant had fled indoors, for the eerie silence that held sway was only occasionally broken by the loud barking of a dog.

'Well, there is our church,' said I, impatiently stamping my feet. 'Are we to return to The Leas and make some headway with this case, Holmes? Remember a girl has been abducted and this seems hardly the time to stand about admiring the view!'

'My dear Watson, I think we should not abandon our country ramble just yet, but rather press on and knock up the vicar.'

I confess my friend's rather obtuse methods often left me quite out at sea, but I had nonetheless learnt from first-hand experience never to dismiss them off-hand.

The rectory was a bleak house of grey Chilmark stone, lightened here and there by clinging ivy and lichen. The garden, like the churchyard, appeared unkempt and neglected.

'Hum – we are being observed from the downstairs window,' said Holmes. 'Careful, my dear Watson; for the present, let us pretend we are a couple of cheery clerks from Leadenhall Street, enjoying a well-earned holiday from our ledgers, who, quite by chance, have happened to encounter this picturesque church!'

'I believe I understand your drift,' said I, and together, with a rather naive spring to our heels, we approached the entrance porch and rang the bell.

There was a short delay and when the door opened, I confess, I momentarily lost my nerve, for the freakish individual who greeted us could quite easily have been mistaken for a corpse. Gaunt of feature and deathly pale, he possessed a stoat-like slanting forehead, adorned by a crop of thinning white hair. White bushy eyebrows hovered above a pair of transparent pink eyes that darted shrewdly between Holmes and myself.

I realised, however, that old age and infirmity were not responsible for this fellow's ghastly white condition but, rather, a defective pigment inherited from birth, for he was an albino!

The cleric wore a black cassock and, surprisingly, despite the bitterly cold weather, only a pair of sandals. He had a leather thong strung around his neck, with a stone dangling from it.

'Good-day,' said my companion, with a good deal of sympathy. 'We were passing your lovely church earlier and wondered if we might take a look around. The drip-stones and crockets are absolutely capital and if you have some stone coffin-covers inside, why, my holiday should be made complete!'

'Really?' The ashen-faced vicar seemed somewhat taken aback by my friend's enthusiasm, however, he regarded us once more with those queer pink eyes of his and answered: 'You are evidently a gentleman who speaks with some authority upon the subject of church architecture though, I fear, a tour of my church is, at present, out of the question. Alas, the doors are all locked up and it appears that Giles, my ancient and absent-minded sexton, has gone to purchase wine at Stow Lynton and taken the keys with him. He is such a forgetful old fellow. What a pity!' He clasped his hands together, raising his eyes heavenward, feigning piety.

However, once the vicar realised we had no intention of being put off quite so easily, he chose not to abandon Christian charity altogether!

'Well, the church aside, gentlemen, perhaps you would care to join me in my study for a blast of fire – after all, it is so devilishly chilly out here!'

'That would be most kind,' said Holmes, taking a backward glance at the chancel wall before we went inside.

The vicar led us along a gloomy, oak-panelled passage to his study. The room was a veritable mausoleum of dusty old books and queer religious artefacts. A crackling log fire burnt in the grate and sporadic gusts of wood smoke, blown about by the wind whistling across the chimneys, occasionally filled the room. The cleric chose one of several long-stemmed clays, previously filled with tobacco from a rack upon the mantelpiece, and lit it.

He fell into his easy chair and proceeded to smoke the pipe with evident relish, all the while gazing dreamily at my companion who was perusing the many dusty leather-bound volumes that lined the walls.

'A most singular collection of antiquarian books, if I might say so!'

The anaemic cleric drew on his pipe and nodded.

'I read mostly on winter nights, Sir. I must confess that I find certain of their number rather stimulating!'

'But some of these volumes are extremely rare,' my companion insisted. 'Guenebault's, *Le re'veil de L'antique tombeau de chyndonat*, or Elias Schedis, *De dis Germanis!* That is surely a collector's classic?'

'Oh, really!' The vicar blew out some smoke and with a glazed look declared sleepily, 'They were passed down to me by my dear old Welsh grandmother. I was stuck with a trunk-load of the things and could not bring myself to part with them. I could have burnt the literature, I suppose, but, I decided to read it all instead!'

Holmes replaced the volume on the shelf, went over to the mantelpiece and stood listening to the wind whistling energetically about the chimney.

'I take it your congregation is a small one?' he asked.

'My dear Sir,' the cleric answered, staring at the glow from the blackened bowl of his pipe, 'on Sundays I sometimes have a congregation of twelve. In the winter months I mostly take in old Roy and he has to do. He's a friendly enough old fellow and seems to like my sermons well enough!'

'Old Roy is your manservant, I take it?' said I.

'No, Sir, he is my mastiff! I think you can hear him barking upstairs now,' he said with a shriek of laughter. 'Anyhow, I am a bachelor and my interests are purely scholarly. I do not abhor solitude – on the contrary, I embrace it, for here, amongst my books I am free to strengthen my faith and contemplate the mysteries of God. My parish is a small one, I grant you, and, yet, I compliment myself on having an excellent spiritual rapport with the parishioners.'

'I see,' said Holmes. 'Well, perhaps we should not detain you further?'

The vicar seemed not unduly concerned at our departure, and as we prepared to leave his manners were Christian enough. However, I confess my medical impartiality to his loathsome white condition was severely tested when I caught a fleeting glimpse of his ghostly semblance staring at me from the mirror – the pupils of his eyes much pin-pricked due to the initial influence of opium.

We returned to The Leas at around two o'clock and there, leaning upon the garden gate, admiring the abundant winter flora thereabouts, was Professor Kempe. The Professor was a wiry individual with a kindly face. He possessed a bronzed, well-travelled complexion, which contrasted pleasingly with his glittering blue eyes and shock of grizzled white hair swept back from his forehead. I should have said he purchased his boots from Lobbs and frequented the finest city tailors, for he dressed immaculately, although, for some reason, he sported a Turkish fez with a tassel dangling from it, which seemed strangely incongruous with the rest of his gear.

We went inside the cottage where Mister Ragthorne's wife had kindly prepared a dinner and afterwards sat with our pipes and talked.

'Professor,' said my companion, at length, 'You are a numismatist of considerable renown and a member of the British Numismatist Society. I should like you to examine this coin.'

Holmes placed the coin he had found face upwards

upon the deal table and, relighting his old briar, lounged in an armchair by the hearth.

'A bronze medallion,' the Professor commented, gruffly. 'Obverse, the profile of the eighteenth-century antiquarian, William Sturkey, and upon the reverse a distinctive engraving of the prehistoric monument, Stonehenge. He was interested in the ancient Celts I believe, and wrote several manuscripts on the subject.'

'Just so. And what of the condition?'

'Although a little oxidised, the coin is in excellent condition. I should imagine it has been subjected to the elements for only a short time. One of a collection of tokens, presumably belonging to a person of antiquarian interests. A remarkable specimen!'

'Professor, another reason why I specifically asked you to come here is because in academic circles, at least, you are regarded as something of an authority on the ancient Celts. I recall you wrote a controversial article about Stonehenge in *The Times* last year. Perhaps you would care to elaborate?'

'I should be delighted,' the spritely old fellow replied, with the gusto of a man a score and ten years younger than he was. 'According to relevant classical and vernacular sources, the most prolific date in the calendar of Stonehenge is the twenty-first of June – the summer solstice. After much long and painstaking research, I concluded that the actual pinnacle of the megalithic calendar is, in fact, diametrically opposite – that is, the winter solstice when the setting sun shall be seen just to the left of the tallest stone, which was once the opening between the two uprights of the great central trilithon. It is the sunset as opposed to sunrise that was the great Celtic celebration here – not simply a fertility rite embracing the dawn but rather a crude druidic festival aimed solely at worshipping the setting sun, which in turn heralds the darkness and the risen moon.'

'Moon worship?' said I, tentatively. 'Surely that is associated with the devil?'

'The devil has a rather medieval ring about it, Doctor Watson. Remember we are going back much further in time. But, yes, that the druids, with their sacrificial practices, had great powers and greater knowledge of the stars cannot be doubted. The sacrifice of the first born or young virgins formed the very nexus of an ancient religious cult.'

'Your reference to sunrise and sunset, light and darkness, thereby good and evil, is perfectly clear. However, have you any real evidence to substantiate this primitive race of moon worshippers actually carried out such deplorable acts of ritual slaughter?' I asked.

'At Woodhenge – not lying far from Stonehenge, Doctor Watson, evidence is forthcoming of the savage demands of this primitive religion. Buried in the axis of the internal sanctuary, the skeleton of a baby was discovered whose head had been cleft open with an axe when it was offered as a sacrifice.'

'But all this controversial theorising about a pile of stones leads us nowhere, Holmes! What of Clara? Surely she should be our primary concern here?'

'Clara is being kept prisoner inside the church, my dear Watson!'

'Good lord, Holmes, how on earth did you deduce that?'

'There were a number of useful indicators. That rather limp excuse about the absent-minded sexton having gone off to Stow Lynton with the church keys being one of them!'

'Why do you say that?'

'My dear man, did you not hear them for yourself? The keys jangling in the pocket of his cassock, I mean? And, talking of cassocks, the vicar's had a piece of black cloth torn from the hem!'

'Of course – the rusty nail on the old timber stile!' I ejaculated.

'And, the coin, Watson. Let us not forget the bronze medallion. No doubt this was accidentally mislaid when the vicar abducted the girl. However, let us presume for argument's sake that Clara left the cottage of her own free will. If this was the case, why? Perhaps she had a passing acquaintance with whoever came to visit her on that afternoon?'

'The vicar is the perfect candidate,' said I.

'A person to be trusted, Watson, and who knows, with a contrite manner and a gift for persuasion ... but, let us pass on to a far more perplexing aspect of this case. For I perceive this cold-blooded scoundrel, the vicar of Upper Wexham, is a devotee of De-Quincy and has a peculiar penchant for reading antiquarian literature concerning magical lore and the black arts. I believe him to be, in reality, an arch-druid, perhaps of some wayward order, who has, under the auspices of broadening one's spiritual outlook, converted his entire flock to paganism! Would you be good enough to inform us of today's date, Professor Kempe?'

'Yes, of course, it is December the twenty-first!'

'And, that is—'

'The date of the winter solstice. I thought you were aware of that, Mister Holmes!'

'Then, it is upon this very day Clara is to be sacrificed!'

'The evening light is already fading,' said I. 'We must hurry, Holmes!'

'My dear Watson, a girl's life hangs in the very balance! One rash, else ill-thought out move could place her life in considerable jeopardy! Professor Kempe, your knowledge of Stonehenge and of the druidic ceremony itself could prove invaluable. Might I ask at which point you consider it prudent to infiltrate their number and rescue the girl?'

'It is quite simple,' said he, adjusting his spectacles, 'for as the sun sets low in the sky all the attention of the worshippers, without exception, shall be focused upon the tallest stone. You must approach from behind and catch them off-guard while their backs are turned. There is a ditch surrounding the Aubrey Stones and this should provide adequate cover, although the place is so exposed it will be a risky business!'

And so, upon that bright and chilly December afternoon, as the expanse of reddening sky above the plains merged with mauvish, silvery clouds, our party – which consisted of the genial Professor, Mister Ragthorne, his son, Edward, and ourselves – rattled along the road to Shrewton and Devizes in a four-wheeler.

I meditated upon these broad Wiltshire acres and it seemed to me the air was alive with the restless spirits of our ancestors. Who were this strange cult of megalithic builders whose graves archaeologists had so freely plundered in the past, I wondered? What if my own eternal rest should, one day, be disturbed and my skull and bones unearthed and imprisoned in some glass museum case?

These grim meanderings were mercifully interrupted when our carriage came to an abrupt halt. There, in the distance, I saw Stonehenge, the solitary circle of stones wreathed in a thin haze of smoky vapour. The uprights stood like some vast gallows, with the blood-red orb of the sun slowly sinking behind.

'The ceremony has already begun!' cried the Professor.

And, indeed, it had, for we could hear the slow monotonous chant of voices and the steady tramp of feet beating out a devilish pagan tattoo upon the ancient ground. The smoke rising from the druids' torches blew about the stones and concealed our movements admirably.

It was not long before we managed to crawl on our bellies to the outer perimeter ditch. We were armed with only Holmes's cane, Mister Ragthorne's old blunder-buss and my service revolver and, yet, I was certain we possessed stout enough hearts and a firm resolve to bring about a successful conclusion to our perilous endeavours.

'Watson, it is time. See they are about to turn and face the tallest stone! Now let us advance towards the Saracen Ring!'

We crept out of the ditch and made our way round the first group of stones and, thereafter, stood behind a huge boulder. I observed the many hooded figures robed like some devilish monks drifting in and out of the smoke, their flaming torches emitting a foul-smelling malodorous fug.

Clara lay in the midst of this fetid crew, pinioned to the altar like some poor wounded bird. The corpse-like, anaemic figure of the vicar of Upper Wexham was leering down at her, a long-bladed knife held in his grasp. The white-faced villain was about to strike the blade home!

The sun slowly sank behind the tallest stone, blanketing Stonehenge with an eerie blood-red glow.

We had no bugle boy but with a loud bang from Mister Ragthorne's blunder-buss as our war-cry we charged into the ring. Much confusion followed and many of the druids, perhaps mistaking us for a crowd of spectral Neolithic men arisen from the numerous burial mounds common to the vicinity, ran for their lives! I wondered at these ordinary folk dressed up so ridiculously, perhaps the village post-master and the sexton amongst them.

My colleague, using his long, thin cane as a martial implement, delivered a couple of masterly blows to the vicar's knuckles and sent the knife scuttling across the ground.

Whilst Holmes seized a length of cord from around the cleric's waist and bound his wrists tightly together I clamped my service revolver against the fiend's temple. He screamed unspeakable oaths and ranted on about how we had prevented him from fulfilling his life's work, but regardless we bundled him over to the four-wheeler where, as pre-arranged, Inspector Tullet and a company of police officers from the Wiltshire Constabulary were waiting to receive him.

Perhaps there was some glimmer of satisfaction to be had from having apprehended the villain, but it was nothing to the immense pleasure I felt whereupon, bundling the fellow away, I saw Clara once more reunited with her dear relations, free, at last, from the evil machinations of the arch-druid, the Reverend Thomas Llewellyn, M.A.

Incidentally, the obese miscreant, young Carker, mentioned earlier in this narrative, whose name I have deliberately changed for reasons of discretion, took ship to South Africa as a stowaway and eventually ended up owning one of the largest mines for mineral deposits in the country. He is, I believe, now a millionaire many times over.

5

The Mysterious Death of Emily Woodcock

It so happened that on a sunny spring afternoon we were strolling down South Audley Street, discussing a lunch-time concert of Paganini's violin concerto and my friend, Mister Sherlock Holmes was, I think, explaining the high standard of technique required to play certain passages, whereupon, turning the corner of Berkeley Square the most tragic circumstance occurred. A distraught woman, in middle years, wearing a navy-blue dress with a light summer coat draped across her shoulders staggered down a flight of steps and clutching at her throat collapsed upon the pavement in front of one of the magnificent Georgian terraced houses.

At that same instant a constable came running along the street, blowing his whistle.

We dashed across the square and I immediately set to work. Any attempt at resuscitation, however, proved to be no more than a formality.

'She is quite dead, Holmes,' said I, feeling for a non-existent pulse and gently drawing the lids across the woman's sightless, staring eyes.

Thereafter, a handsome young gentleman of about four and thirty came out on to the porch. He wore a dark frock-coat with a gold repeater and watch-chain dangling from the pocket.

'Can I be of any assistance?' he asked in a rather brash manner, waving me aside.

'I think everything is perfectly in order,' said I.

'I am a doctor, Sir! Now, get out of my way and let me examine this woman!'

'That will not be necessary,' I answered, a little tetchily, 'for, I am myself a doctor!'

'My dear Sir,' he said, apologetically, 'I did not mean to appear conceited. Doctor Aubrey, Harley Street.' He put his hand out and I shook it.

'Doctor Watson. I have a small practice in Paddington,' I replied.

He evidently recognised the deceased and tenderly placed his hand upon her forehead.

'What on earth has happened here? Has there been an accident?' he said.

'She has suffered a fatal seizure,' said I, shielding my eyes from the glare of the mid-day sun.

'Why, that is preposterous!' The doctor grew exceedingly pale. 'I only examined her myself a short while ago!'

I left Holmes bent over the corpse with his magnifying lens, the constable standing beside him, and, taking Doctor Aubrey's arm walked across the pavement beneath the shade afforded by the portico of number 39 Berkeley Mansions, where we took stock of events.

'You left your patient unattended!' said I, gruffly,

for in my own mind I had formed that same conclusion.

'My dear Sir,' he replied, considerably hurt by the remark. 'It so happens I have several patients in this house who form part of my round. I attended Emily Woodcock and, afterwards, went upstairs to visit Sir Charles Fairweather in the apartment above. Am I to be struck off the Medical Register for that, Doctor Watson?'

'Not at all,' I half apologised. 'But, I must mention that before she collapsed your patient seemed hysterical and this gives me cause for grave concern.'

'Hysterical?' He seemed puzzled by this remark. 'Why, when I last saw Emily she was perfectly composed, sat at her desk dealing with her correspondence.'

'I thought, perhaps you had informed her she was suffering from a fatal illness of some kind. Patients often react differently to this intelligence. Some accept it with a serene composure, others need to be restrained and comforted.'

'My patient has had for some months a cartilaginous tumour of the parathyroid gland, however, this was not malignant and there was never any question of surgery. She complained of stomach pains and a little nausea earlier.'

The constable had evidently been listening to our conversation for he butted in,

'And, perfectly understandable that the lady should have done so under the circumstances!'

'What are you getting at?' said I, not much liking the black look he was giving Doctor Aubrey.

'Mister Holmes is of the opinion that the woman

was killed by a lethal dose of poison and, as a consequence, I must ask you to accompany me to Scotland Yard, Doctor Aubrey.'

'Now look here,' said I, coming to the young fellow's assistance. 'This man is a Harley Street physician!'

The policeman, no doubt over-eager to win promotion in the Force, ignored my reasonable protestations entirely, and was about to seize Aubrey when he shoved the officer aside and legged it across the public lawn. He must have been a hundred-yard sprinter, for no one could catch him. With bounding athletic strides he made it to the corner of Berkeley Square and was gone.

Holmes, meanwhile, joined me and lit a cigarette. The incident evidently amused him.

'Young Aubrey was about to be arrested!' I said, somewhat aggrieved by my friend's indifference to the outrage of a gentleman being accused of such a crime.

'It is, of course, quite natural that you should side with a professional colleague, Watson!'

'Do you actually mean to say she was murdered, Holmes?' said I, somewhat incredulously.

'She died after being administered a lethal dose of poison. Did you not observe the skin dis-colouration and the fact she had vomited recently? I think Wyndam, the pathologist at Charing Cross Hospital will bear me out on that point. Oh, and another trifle, Watson; it seems hardly coincidence that when she ran down the steps there happened to be a constable coming down the street towards her.'

Inspector Brown arrived on the scene shortly after and accompanied by an old bow-legged house-porter, sporting a drab plum-coloured frock-coat, trimmed with gold buttons and ornamental braid, we were led upstairs and shown into the dead woman's apartment.

Emily Woodcock was apparently the widow of the tea millionaire, Sir Alistair Woodcock, and wholly consistent with a man who had worked his way up from barrow-boy to becoming one of the foremost wholesale suppliers of bulk and packet tea in Great Britain, the place was elegantly furnished with all the trappings familiar to wealth and affluence. Fifteenth-century Flemish paintings by Van Eyck and Weyden graced the walls of the spacious drawing room and a Rubens hung above the fireplace. There was a grand piano heaped with family portraits, the largest being a ravishing picture of the widow and next to it, a young cricketer in Westminster School colours, who, according to the porter was the tea millionaire's son by his previous marriage: Morston Wellby Woodcock, now grown up and proprietor of the Bond Street picture gallery Horabys.

To coincide with what Doctor Aubrey had told me earlier, facing the west window was a bureaux filled with all the usual paraphernalia, including bottles of ink, business documents, a paper knife, string, sealing wax and so on. On top of the bureaux, I observed a box of Liberty's stationery, recently opened, and next to this a pile of letters, addressed in a neat and meticulous hand awaiting despatch. A single envelope not properly sealed, with the letter still inside, had fallen on to the carpet and unbeknown to Brown, Holmes bent down and discreetly placed it in his pocket.

We did not stay long. I vaguely recall watching from an upstairs window as the crowd dispersed and the corpse was removed by hearse from Berkeley Square. We returned to Baker Street and whilst I spent the remainder of the day catching up with my notes, for the most part working alone in my room, Holmes sat at his desk, engrossed in some chemistry experiment the nature of which I could not determine.

After dinner, I settled down before the fire and continued with my writing. The weather outside had turned and was now wet and cheerless, with the rain monotonously drumming against the window pane.

I suspected few people should be abroad on such a foul night and was, therefore, surprised when at about a quarter past nine I heard a cab rattle to a standstill outside 221b.

Shortly after, the bell clanged and there was the sound of a woman's laughter. I imagined it was one of Mrs Hudson's cronies until I heard footfalls upon the stair.

The door opened and an elegantly dressed young lady entered the room. She shook her brolly and gazed rather earnestly at my colleague. I thought I vaguely recognised her from somewhere.

I mentioned something about the weather and directed the young lady to the sofa.

'Ha, good evening, Doctor Aubrey,' Holmes said, with a chuckle, tossing his newspaper aside.

I was astounded, for sans wig and theatrical make-up, I realised it was none other than young Aubrey, the very man the police were after.

'I am so sorry to call at this hour, dressed like this, gentlemen! I must appear like some girl from the Haymarket!'

'Not at all, Doctor Aubrey! In fact, may I be the first to compliment you on your elegance of posture? I, myself, employ a similar Beaumonde guise on occasions and, I must say, you carry it off very well! Would you prefer coffee or a glass of something stronger?'

'Oh, a whisky and soda,' said he, relaxing a little and wiping his face with a handkerchief. 'Pray, do not mince words, Mister Holmes, am I to be branded a murderer alongside such notorieties in my profession as Smethurst and Pritchard?'

'As you are no doubt aware, the deceased happens to be the widow of Sir Alistair Woodcock, the tea millionaire. Perhaps the police suspect you of some intrigue involving her fortune, although Watson here has stuck by you all along. I tend to be rather more clinical and detached in these matters. After all, you were the last person to see her alive and, as a medical practitioner, had ample opportunity to administer the poison over a period of time and finally prescribe the fatal dose.'

'My dear Sir!' the doctor protested.

Holmes raised his hand to silence him.

'The police are convinced of your guilt. I, on the other hand, promise that by tomorrow noon you shall be above suspicion.' Holmes held out a manila envelope. It was unsealed and addressed to a Miss Beatrice Lorne, Windy Knook, Seaview Drive, Bungay, Suffolk. 'And here is part of the evidence!'

'I have not the slightest idea who Beatrice Lorne is, Mister Holmes, but if this letter can, somehow, save me from the gallows then so be it!'

'Oh, it shall,' replied my colleague, indicating that Aubrey should pass the envelope over to me. I confess I could make little of it, especially when I read the contents. The letter merely contained a few lines touching upon such homely topics as embroidery and the watering of house plants.

'And here is another crucial link in the chain.'

Holmes handed me a wire, received that same afternoon, at our rooms in Baker Street. It read as follows:

Mr S. Holmes.
Sir, remember with some affection your part in the recovery of the stolen 'WEYDON' some years back. Enclosed names as requested.
Sincerely, C. BARTLETT.
Room XVII.
KINGSWOOD, I.R. (Mr)
TATTENHAM, G. (Mr)
SMITH, O. (Mrs)
GOODMAN, S. (Mr)
CHIPSTEAD, M. (Miss)

'Now, if Doctor Aubrey would take the sofa for the night, Watson, I propose that tomorrow morning we pay a visit to the National Gallery, where I shall endeavour to prove, beyond a shadow of doubt, that our friend here is innocent!'

After breakfast we hailed a four-wheeler to Trafalgar Square. The rain of the previous night had ceased altogether. It was a lovely spring morning and as we rattled round the corner of South Africa House, the bright sunshine made the bronze group of fountains in the pigeon-filled square, over-shadowed by Nelson's monument and the imposing spire of Saint Martin-in-the-Fields, glisten delightfully.

Once we had reached our intended destination, Holmes instructed young Aubrey, now more suitably attired in a set of my old cast-offs, to remain outside on the steps and await our return.

We entered the portals of the National Gallery and, there in the forbidding entrance hall, opposite the main publications stall, Holmes immediately seized the sleeve of the attendant and demanded to know the whereabouts of Room XVII. The room was apparently 'out of bounds' to the general public and he adamantly refused to take us there.

However, the arrival of another more senior fellow, attracted by all the commotion and raised voices, smoothed our passage admirably, for my colleague had only to mention the name of C. Bartlett, the gallery's resident expert on Flemish painting, and we were immediately whisked through a side entrance and downstairs to the lower ground floor, where pillaged Old Masters from countless campaigns were cleaned and restored. Here, amongst a labyrinth of corridors, we finally hit upon Room XVII.

The door was ajar, and the room reeked of turpentine and paint. A group of persons clad in artists' smocks and overalls were diligently employed behind individual easels, some partially hidden from view by screens.

'Mildred Chipstead?' said Holmes, in a loud assertive voice, addressing no one in particular.

A pretty brunette, wearing a jeweller's eye-glass, scraping away with a scalpel at the bottom right-hand panel of a portrait by Van Eyck of a man wearing a turban turned round and nodded. Her colleagues remained busily absorbed in their work and did not pay us the slightest attention.

'Madeleine, actually!' she replied, removing her eye-glass. 'Are you come from Windsor and Newton? I asked for a set of fine camel-haired brushes the other day and you sent me the wrong ones!'

'Alas, I am not a stationery clerk but a consulting detective, Madam! I apologise for this wretched inconvenience,' my companion said cheerily, taking off his hat, 'but I must ask you a few questions concerning Emily Woodcock. I only hold out the vaguest hope that these trifling enquiries might, somehow, determine the whereabouts of young Doctor Aubrey.'

'The man the police are after?'

'Just so. Scotland Yard have had little luck so far and what with one thing and another I have had quite a busy night of it, I'm afraid. You are connected to the family, I take it?'

'Yes, of course!' the young lady replied, placing her scalpel on the workbench beside her. 'Morston Woodcock is my fiancé, and we are to be married next month. He informed me of his step-mother's unfortunate demise yesterday evening, and is quite distraught over the affair.'

'Do you specialise in early Flemish?'

'The department deals with a wide spectrum of paintings from the collection.'

'And, you undertook to restore a Van Eyck from Emily Woodcock's late husband's private collection, did you not?'

'Why, yes, *The Child at the Foot of the Temple.* How did you know?'

'Elementary! A simple message scribbled across the cover of a rather dog-eared copy of a penny guide to the National Gallery. I have it here as a matter of fact. Shall I read it to you? "Sunday morning, April tenth. Removed old varnish from every lineament of child's face and toga. Emily, when you return from the Abbey please find packet of Liberty's stationery, as requested, on top of bureaux, M.C." You are the "M.C." referred to here, I take it?' Holmes bent over and glanced at her exercise book, resting on the easel. 'Ah, yes, I can see from your notes that the writing corresponds perfectly!'

'And, where did you find this penny guidebook?'

'Clasped in the hand of the dead woman! An odd place for it to end up, I know, but there we are. Such a fine collection of paints,' said Holmes, stepping over to the bench. 'So many different shades of colour to choose from and, pray, what does this bottle, separate from the rest, contain? Shall I open it?' he said, picking up a bottle of white powder and unscrewing the cap.

'Ordinary paint!'

'On the contrary, Madam, this bottle contains a quantity of crystalline salts, and what of the vase over there? My, you have been extremely lax!'

'Some water to rinse my brushes!' she answered, becoming increasingly wary of her visitor.

Holmes took out an envelope from his pocket and waved it gently in front of her beautiful face like a Chinese fan.

'I admire you for your ingenuity, Madam. Alas, I must condone the crime!'

My companion carefully unfolded the envelope. I never saw such a change come over a woman's face.

'And, here is the proof!'

There was a loud rap at the door.

'Ah, Brown, I see you received my wire.'

'We have arrested Doctor Aubrey, Mister Holmes! He was brazenly sunning himself on the steps outside. Why are you looking at me like that?'

'Because, Brown, Doctor Aubrey was not the person I had intended you to arrest!'

'But, the wire – it was plain enough!'

'I am afraid I must inform you that the murderer of Emily Woodcock was none other than the woman who stands before you now.'

'You have the evidence then?'

'Waddon, the forensic expert at the Yard, will, I am sure, verify my findings. Here, take this!'

'An envelope? Come now, Mister Holmes, surely this is a little trite!'

'On the contrary, this envelope will tell you everything, as it did me, but let us firstly consider young Aubrey's part in the affair. The doctor examined his patient and as is often so in cases of poisoning, the symptoms so closely resemble those of natural disease that he did not suspect there was anything amiss. Given that Emily Woodcock was writing her letters when Doctor Aubrey last saw her before going upstairs to visit another patient, we must therefore surmise that at some stage she slipped the letters into corresponding envelopes. There were, I believe, twelve letters awaiting despatch upon her bureaux. The thirteenth I found lying on the carpet. You will observe it is open and I have it in my possession here.'

'Well, what does the letter inside say, then?' the Inspector said impatiently.

'We shall ignore the letter,' Holmes answered. 'The envelope on the other hand is of primary significance. Emily Woodcock apparently did not lick the gum and seal it, and with good reason I think, because she was suddenly seized with acute stomach pains. Why then, despite being in considerable agony, instead of alerting her physician on the floor above, did she go over to the window and, upon seeing a constable on the other side of the street some hundred yards or so distant, rush downstairs?'

'She realised she had been poisoned!' said I.

'Precisely, Watson, and more important, she wished to communicate to the constable the name of the person she strongly suspected had administered the poison to her. Alas she never had the chance to do so.'

'That person's name was Doctor Aubrey,' Brown butted in. 'Why bother with all this long-winded preamble, Mister Holmes? It is a foregone conclusion, and an obvious one!'

'And mistaken!' Holmes rebuffed the detective

with a wag of his finger. 'We must firstly apply ourselves to the problem of how the poison was originally administered. I propose that Morston Wellby Woodcock purchased a box of Liberty's stationery from the department store in Regent Street. A liaison with his fiancée followed and Miss Chipstead returned to the gallery. In this very department, possibly whilst her colleagues were still at lunch, she knowingly tampered with the contents.'

'A lie!' The pretty brunette almost spat out the words. 'How dare you slander my future husband in this way!'

'And, notwithstanding, skilfully applied a solution of antimony, an odourless, white crystalline salt, soluble in water, to the strip of gum along the edge of each individual envelope, with a paint brush. On Sunday last, Miss Chipstead visited Emily Woodcock's flat in Berkeley Square to restore one of the Van Eyck paintings belonging to her late husband's private collection. But, of course, she had another purpose in mind, for as prearranged with her fiancé, she carefully placed the box of stationery on top of the bureaux. Both must have, no doubt, been aware that at some stage Emily, a voracious letter writer, would use the envelopes and, more importantly, seal them!'

'And therefore with every lick of her tongue she unwittingly hastened her own end,' said I.

'And remember, death did not occur instantaneously but rather the poison was gradually absorbed into her system.'

'My God, you have ruined everything!' the

98

despicable woman said, admonishing my companion with a fierce glance.

'Incidentally, I arranged with Inspector Brown here for your fiancé to be apprehended this morning at his gallery in Bond Street, and taken to Scotland Yard. He shall have a great deal of explaining to do, I think!'

'But, what of the motive?' I asked, wondering what kind of twisted reasoning could have possibly driven two respectable and otherwise comfortably-off persons to murder their own kin.

'Greed, my dear Watson! What other motive could there possibly be?' Holmes sighed. 'I recall reading in *The Times* obituary column that the tea millionaire left his entire fortune to his second wife. Upon her death, presumably, that same fortune would pass directly to Alistair Woodcock's son by his previous marriage.'

'Morston Wellby?' said I. 'And the son resented the way in which his step-mother took precedence over himself in his father's affections?'

'That would appear to be the case,' Holmes agreed. 'Although, if I remember correctly, there were peculiar circumstances surrounding the death of his mother, a one-time variety hall artist, who died suddenly after tasting a cup of her husband's specially blended tea.'

'My dear Holmes!'

'I shall not elaborate!' he protested. 'However, might I suggest we take lunch at Simpsons and, afterwards, visit Covent Garden for a stimulating performance of Donizetti's *Lucrezia Borgia*: the scene where Gennaro is poisoned is quite a poignant spectacle, I hear.'

6

The Silver Button

There had for some time been a passing fad in the science of phrenology, that is the theory that definite criminal types can be identified by the shape of their cranium. One morning I decided to consult Holmes, upon certain cranial characteristics beholden to a South London chimney sweep, recently arrested and accused of the brutal murder of the meat and poultry millionaire, Henry Clanthorpe.

'Holmes,' said I, 'I must intrude upon your rashers and egg and beg you to consider this portrait in the *Telegraph*.'

He snatched the newspaper and propped it up in front of the coffee pot.

'Albert Locke, the chimney sweep,' answered he, with some petulance, scarcely bothering to look at it.

'You will observe the prominent forehead, curly thinning hair and, in particular, the bumps noticeable upon the left-hand side of his skull – a murderous specimen if ever I saw one!'

My companion begged to differ.

'My dear Watson, he possesses a square type of

head we often associate with Teutonic people. A small, weak face exudes a certain childish naivety and the lips are indicative of baser passions, though I should not place too much importance upon his cranium if I were you.'

The meal finished, Holmes fell upon the sofa, lit his after-breakfast pipe and browsed over the agony column in *The Times*. I took my coffee over to the arm-chair and, gazing out of the bow window, rested my eye upon the shadowy frontages of the houses opposite, vaguely visible through the blanket of dun-coloured fog.

Barely had I put cup to saucer when a carriage rattled to a standstill outside 221b. Shortly after there occurred a loud and persistent knock at the front door.

'Ah, Brown,' Holmes murmured from behind a thick fug of rank tobacco smoke. 'The scrape of his shoe upon the pavement where the studs are defective is always a giveaway!'

There was a brief confusion of voices and I heard footfalls rapidly approaching upon the stair.

'Inspector Brown,' said my colleague, before ever the door was opened. 'A chilly morning. Do please come in and share a blast of fire! You must be frozen.'

The door to our apartment opened timidly and there, just as my companion had predicted, was the Scotland Yard detective, hat held almost penitently in hand.

'My dear Brown, after the arrest of the chimney sweep, I should have thought you would be strutting around like a peacock this morning; instead, I find you severely out of sorts and walking about with a slouch. You have not slept well, I take it, and are caught in a quandary: a clear-cut case, or, is the man you have recently taken into custody in fact the wrong one?And then there is the trifling matter of Clanthorpe's body.'

Brown did not, at first, reply, but warmed himself in front of the blazing fire. Once the colour had returned to his cheeks, he admitted as much.

'You are, of course, correct, Mister Holmes! I have had a wretched night of it, I'm afraid, we have yet to discover the actual whereabouts of the body!'

'But are you certain the meat and poultry millionaire is dead?' said I.

'By the copious amounts of blood and brains spread over the Turkey carpet in front of the hearth in Clanthorpe's study, I should say no man could have survived such a ferocious attack, Doctor Watson.'

Holmes's eyes glittered as he struck a match to his pipe and watched a ring of tobacco smoke slowly curl up towards the ceiling. 'Apparently, the sweep spent the evening drinking beer at the Kestral public house, on the corner of Brick Lane and the murder was committed somewhere between half-past midnight and the early hours of Tuesday morning, Clanthorpe's residence on Northalt Avenue being only across the street from there. A considerable amount of soot was discovered by the police upon the carpet and, most importantly, the French dresser, where the plate was kept under lock and key. By some unfortunate coincidence, Albert Locke happened to visit the Clanthorpe residence earlier that day, to clean the chimneys and flues, did he not?'

'Yes,' I said. 'The police have it that the perfect opportunity presented itself for the chimney sweep to look around the house and plan the burglary for later that night.'

'However, this argument is to my mind, at least, by no means flawless!'

Holmes reclined upon the sofa, part of his face lit up by the dim, reflected radiance of the fire, and remarked, 'The case is a curious one! I think, perhaps, a visit to Brixton is in order. Are you game, Watson?'

'I should be delighted!' said I.

Clanthorpe's residence in Northalt Avenue was a pleasant Georgian-styled house, backed to the north with a rosy brick wall and steep railway embankment. A gravel path led directly to a flight of granite steps, upon which stood the entrance porch. There was easy access into the back garden by means of a tall trellis gate at the side of the house.

The front door stood partly ajar and we entered the meat and poultry millionaire's residence – rather a modest dwelling, I might add. A constable instantly recognised Brown and escorted us along the passageway.

The quiet of the place was only disturbed by a big ormolu clock, ticking loudly in the hall.

Holmes took a hurried and furtive glance into the drawing-room. 'Halloa! Paintings all askew,' he confided in a hushed voice. 'A safe was evidently what our friend, the ferret, was after. Dear me, and the sooty marks along the wall – thumb and forefinger, middle and third – just smell the atmosphere, Watson.' Holmes ran the tip of his cane along the skirting board. 'A ghastly murder was perpetrated in this very house. A man bludgeoned to death and yet the police have still to find the body: capital!'

'Here is the study, Mister Holmes,' said Brown, dismissing the constable with a wave of his hand.

We passed into a sparsely furnished room. There was a considerable amount of blood on the carpet and splashed along the wall to the left of the fireplace. But what interested my colleague was a set of French windows that led straight out into the garden.

The lock and latch had been crudely forced and as a direct consequence flecks of glass and paint lay strewn about the floor beneath. A window pane had been cracked along its entire length.

'The means of entry,' said Brown, carefully enclosing his fingers around the brass door knob and opening it for us.

'And also a means of exit!' replied Holmes, briskly stepping out on to the patio and taking a breath of fresh air. 'I shall not be a moment, Watson,' said he. 'I intend to take a little stroll down to the end of the garden and admire some of those winter roses running along the boundary wall.'

Shortly afterwards we heard a shrill whistle. I glanced out of the French windows and observed a passenger train slowly clatter along the embankment. The carriages disappeared around the curve and when the smoke had cleared I observed with some amusement my colleague clamber over the wall at the end of the garden and leap down upon the other side. Thereafter, he appeared at the summit of the embankment, elegantly dressed in his long grey travelling cloak and deer-stalker, leaning upon his cane and looking first one way and then in the direction of Herne Hill.

He returned to the house and proceeded to examine the French dresser where all the plate had been kept. Holmes took up his lens and, spread upon all fours, looked beneath it.

'You'll not find Clanthorpe's body under there, Sir!' said Brown, with an empty laugh.

'No,' replied my friend, getting up and brushing down his coat. 'But, I did come across this little trinket.'

'A silver button!' said I, moving closer.

Brown appeared not to consider it of much importance and instead began to pontificate at some length about the case.

'From what I can gather so far, it appears the sweep left his bull terrier with the landlord at the Kestral and wheeled his barrow across the road to Northalt Avenue. The fog was thick, remember, but Harriet Wimpole, who resides opposite in number 49 observed Clanthorpe pacing to and fro in his dressing gown, smoking a cigarette at eleven. Locke must have crept around the side of the house, unlatched the trellis gate and gained entry by means of the French windows. Shortly after, the intruder was caught red-handed by the old man. A confrontation took place and a murder was committed. Afterwards, the sweep returned by the exact same route he had taken earlier round the side of the house and deposited the body, together with the plate, upon his barrow and wheeled them off, somewhere, perhaps, to the nearby allotment!'

'I must beg to differ,' my friend interrupted. 'At the end of the garden beneath the brick wall, I detected small drops of blood upon the flagstone path and upon the other side of the wall I found this!'

'A silver button, and the exact same shape and size as the other!' said I.

'Well,' said Brown testily, 'you disappoint me, Mister Holmes, for upon the other side of the wall there lies only the embankment and beyond the railway line rows of terraced houses. A man would never be able to carry Clanthorpe's body and the plate that far without considerable difficulty!'

'No, but, if he had an accomplice?'

'Whatever!' the detective replied, becoming rather cocksure of himself. 'The noose looks as good as tied around Albert Locke's neck, for I have it on good authority from the Governor of Pentonville Prison, no less, that the sweep possessed a grubby knee-length coat and upon entering the prison last week two silver buttons were missing from it!'

I have on numerous occasions accompanied Sherlock Holmes on a visit to Pentonville Prison, and as our cab rattled down the Caledonian Road I reflected a little gloomily that Albert Locke, whether guilty or innocent of the crime of murder, remained a captive behind its grim portcullis gates and that my companion was his last hope of reprieve. The weighty evidence the police had amassed against him and the ominous fact that the Clanthorpe Meat and Poultry Company had the services of the eminent Queen's Counsel, Sir Charles Biddlington, for the prosecution did not bode well for the chimney sweep.

I believed his chances of acquittal – for he was due up at the Old Bailey the following Monday – closely resembled those of a blindfolded, one-armed rifleman being requested not only to hit the target but the bull dead centre also!

After a brief consultation with the Governor we were directed to the cell where the prisoner was being kept on remand.

Albert Locke sat upon a rude wooden bench listlessly tugging at the sleeve of his prison clothes. He had barely touched a dinner of soup and potatoes and a more sullen and hopelessly dejected fellow would be hard to imagine.

'I will tell you gentlemen from Lincoln's Inn the same as I did the last,' said he, wearily. 'I am innocent! I never did no lark and I am going to thrash in the pit for a murder I never committed!'

He held his head despairingly in his shackled hands and there in that gloomy cell I, at once, felt a sense of pity, for the look of foreboding upon his face was terrible to behold.

'What is that you have brought?' said he, half-cursing, considering with some contempt the brown paper parcel my colleague had collected from the Governor earlier.

'More tracts and the like, I suppose!' he protested.

'On the contrary,' said Holmes as he unwrapped the parcel. 'I should very much like your opinion upon a small matter concerning this fine, if a little grubby, knee-length coat, Mister Locke.'

'It is an old rag I know, Sir, but it is the only one I have. I bought it from a Jew selling fried fish.'

'Hum – and you will observe that there are two silver buttons missing from it.'

'Perhaps I should get my wife to sew them on one day, if I am still alive and not buried under the lime with felons treading all over me!'

Holmes took the silver buttons from his pocket and placed them against the ones on the sweep's coat. Although cast from the same cheap alloy the difference was immediately evident.

'You will observe, my dear Watson, that these have a reddish-brown thread whereas the slightly smaller buttons fastened to the coat have a delicate green colour.'

'Wrong size!' the sweep remarked, 'though I am very much obliged to you for your charity, Sir.'

'Well, for the present we shall let the matter rest there. I am very much indebted for your time, Mister Locke, good-day!'

'And may I ask your name, Sir?' said he with a puzzled look.

'My name is Sherlock Holmes and this is my colleague, Doctor Watson,' my friend answered as I bashed on the door with my cane to alert the warder that our brief interview had drawn to a close.

We next took the train to Brixton. I imagined we should return to Northalt Avenue, and yet my companion decided to venture further along the line to Herne Hill.

I spent the entire time smoking and gazing out of the window at the long rows of terraced houses. The train rattled to a halt at a stop signal just outside Herne Hill and during the delay as a 'special' thundered past, the red lamp quickly disappearing round the curve, my companion suddenly seized my arm and flung wide the compartment door.

We jumped down on to the bank, waited for the train to move off and trudged along for some thirty yards or so until we came to a corrugated iron shack. There was a sign above the door which read: 'HUT – MILE POST 16 – 19½'.

The door was locked but by means of a small window we managed to clamber inside. The floor was damp and littered with old newspapers and broken clay pipes. Upon the workbench stood a kettle and a rack of tools. Over in a corner I observed a bulky canvas corn bag propped up against some shovels.

Holmes knelt down and passed me a sheet of newspaper. A large brownish oval stain, tinged darker around the edges, was spread over much of the print.

'Blood!' said I.

'And a great deal of it,' said my companion, creeping across to where the shovels lay and brushing his hand against the corn bag.

'The missing plate, Watson! Go careful and let's leave this place just as we found it.'

Shortly after, a train went hurtling past and once it had gone by we started off down the line. It was dark and we could see the lighted windows of the signal box up ahead. As we approached a face peered down at us and a voice shouted out, 'Halloa, there! What is your business on railway property, gentlemen?'

'We are Railway Inspectors!' Holmes snapped at once, establishing his authority.

'Well, you had better come up and have a blast of fire,' said the other. 'Go careful, Sir, for the steps are extremely rickety here – I'll shine my bulls-eye and give you some more light!'

'It's freezing out here,' said Holmes, rubbing his hands together. 'By the way, what is your name, fellow?'

'Mugdon – I am the signalman, Sir,' he replied.

'Well, Mugdon, we have been inspecting the lines and they seem well enough though there is the making of a crack upon the curve at the Brixton end!'

'Come in, gentlemen, and sit beside the fire. Do you want tea? There's plenty in the copper.'

'That would be most kind of you, Mister Mugdon,' said Holmes, rubbing his hands together. 'The bottom ballast under the sleeper should have been laid to a depth of sixteen inches and this direction was not carried through properly. I shall, therefore, have to report the matter. By the way, my name is Lumley, the Chief Mechanical Engineer and this is Mister Smith, the Inspecting Officer.'

'I am glad to make your acquaintance, gentlemen.'

The signalman poured out some tea. A bell-telegraph rang the signal for 'line clear' and Mugdon went over and adjusted a points lever.

'It was foggy last night!' remarked Holmes.

'The fog was severe,' he agreed.

'Was the down-line busy?'

'No more than usual.'

'Do you get many trains past two?'

'A deal of regular goods traffic – though past three, apart from the night-mails, there is only the one train that comes this way.'

'Is it a Terrier Class?'

'Well, it is always same engine, *Weald of Kent*. It arrives at Clapham Junction at around half-past three.'

'What was the name again?'

'*Weald of Kent*. Jeb Parsons is the driver and Eddie, his brother, is the fireman.'

'Isn't that Jeb the character who has the wooden leg – or is it his brother who is the cripple? I never can remember which.'

'Neither, Sir! None of 'em is a cripple that I know of – though Eddie always has a queer habit of winking at you. One of his eyes is a bit dodgy I believe.'

'Well, I think perhaps we have taken up enough of your time already, Mister Mugdon, and there are the points at Herne Hill to be inspected.'

'Of course,' came the reply. 'Well, I shall see you again on the line, no doubt, Mister Lumley and, you also, Mister Smith.'

A train for London Victoria was conveniently stood in the platform at Herne Hill station and we lost no time in finding a compartment. Upon reaching Victoria, we summoned a cab and went straight to Baker Street. After a fine dinner, the cheery blaze and familiar surroundings of our rooms did much to restore my spirits for, in truth, the discovery of 'HUT – MILE POST 16 – 19½' had left me feeling rather low.

'Watson,' my companion said, taking down his old black clay from the rack. 'We are going to have rather a late night of it, I fear!'

'Really,' said I, smoking a cigar and helping myself to a large measure of whisky and soda. 'But, what of Albert Locke, the chimney sweep?'

'What of him?' Holmes answered, striking a match and lighting his pipe. 'My dear fellow, he is due to appear at the Central Criminal Court of the Old Bailey on Monday! And, we have tickets for a performance of Scarlatti at Covent Garden, which I should not miss for the world. Dear me, it is a foggy night!'

Here was another peculiar facet of my friend's character: a cold sense of detachment.

'Yes,' I persisted, 'but who murdered Henry Clanthorpe, given that we discovered the missing plate and a large quantity of blood in that hut, earlier? Are we actually any nearer to solving the mystery?'

'A good deal nearer, Watson, for I have wired Brown and, this very night, we are to rendezvous at Clapham Junction to apprehend the villains concerned!'

That night as our cab rattled through the London streets, the fog was particularly sulphurous and dank. On Battersea Bridge Road the gleaming lamps of the hansoms were tinged a fuzzy hue and the jangle of their bells was peculiarly lost and found.

Holmes remained silent and introspective for the

entire journey, peering languidly out at the fog with his knees drawn tightly up to his chin.

At length we arrived at our destination. There rose the yellow lights of Clapham Junction, the gas lamps situated along the perimeter of a grimy, soot-ridden viaduct above.

Holmes lost no time. He dashed into the station entrance and clambered up a steep flight of granite steps. There, at the far end of the deserted down-platform he pointed with his cane in the direction of the coal staves on the other side of the tracks.

'My dear Watson,' said he, taking my arm, 'the time by the station clock is precisely twenty-five minutes past three. There is precious little time. Have you your service revolver handy?'

'I have it here!' said I.

'Do you observe the box van shunted back along the line over there?'

'Indeed!'

'The engine shall come to a standstill just before the red lamp and we will be there to meet it!'

Concealed by the shadows, we stood upon the plate of the break-van and awaited the Terrier with a thrill of anticipation. The fog hampered visibility but, nonetheless, we could hear its approach. The driver made a full application of the break, applied back-steam and moments later the tank engine loomed out of the fog.

We crept cautiously around the side of the van and watched the fireman clamber off the footplate whilst the driver, with considerable difficulty, managed to haul down a large canvas sack to him. After a good deal of cursing the shorter of the pair, who had a nervous twitching about his left eye, declared in a coarse voice: 'Did I hear mention of an honest fence with lodgings along the Radcliffe Highway? I doubt it!'

'And, how else are we to be rid of the plate?'

'I know of a fellow in Cheapside.'

'And I know a Jew in Fetter Lane!'

'And I know a villain when I see one!' cried Holmes as he sprang forward and seized the fireman by the shirt-collar and threw him forcefully against the engine cab.

Meanwhile I clapped my service revolver against the other's temple.

'Excuse my troubling you, Eddie, but I perceive you are in the possession of a most singular velvet waist-coat which I should like to have a closer look at if I may.'

'What the devil!' The fireman struggled against the vice-like grip of my companion.

'I should keep still if I were you, or else Watson here might feel obliged to blow Jeb's brains out. Talking of knowing people,' said Holmes, matter-of-factly, 'I know of an excellent seamstress in Stepney, Mister Parsons!'

'What do you mean by that?' replied the fireman angrily.

'Dear me, you have a couple of buttons missing. Let me see if these are of any use. Watson, you will observe they are a perfect match and the threads are of the identical coarse fibre! Ah, Inspector Brown, I am glad you managed to get here, eventually!'

'I am a little late on account of an overturned brougham on Battersea Bridge, Mister Holmes.'

'Well, perhaps one of your constables would be kind enough to handcuff these gentlemen. Incidentally, the corn bag over there contains the missing plate, the property of Henry Clanthorpe of Northalt Avenue, Brixton, and you two are both under arrest for his murder! said Holmes.

'Then, so be it, the old man's plate is yours!' said the fireman, indignantly. 'I toiled in Clanthorpe's meat factory for thirteen long year sweating at his pork pies and faggots, filling the old miser's pockets with barely enough wages for bread nor to keep my lodgings!'

'And so you conceived a cunning scheme for revenge!' said Holmes.

'I did, Sir, but all we got in the end was blood on our hands! How many times did I take that train journey from Brixton to Herne Hill and back again, all the while dreaming of how I could, somehow, snatch his fortune. It was well-known that he was a miser and hoarded his money. He never trusted a bank in his life and one spring day I saw from my compartment window the old gentleman sat in his garden, reading the newspaper, and fate decided to smile kindly. For, my brother Jeb had recently been promoted to driver by the London and South Eastern Railway Company and shunted coal back'ards and for'ards along the line. Together we decides to hatch a plot.

'I took a job on the railways as a fireman and was later able to join my brother, working this same route.

'Last Thursday night we took a consignment of coal from Purley to the sheds at Clapham. On the

way, we shunted the locomotive along the embankment directly above Clanthorpe's house and went
about our business. We climbed over the wall and
went straightaway down the garden path to break
in from the rear. I went and dragged the old
gentleman out of bed and took him downstairs
where I questioned him about his fortune and the
whereabouts of the safe. However, the wily old
recluse gave nothing away, so we tied him up and
made a search of the house. Every room we ransacked
but we never found no money or gold!'

'And so you murdered him?' said Holmes.

'At this time, murder was not on our minds, Sir,
although after I had applied the hot poker to his
leg for the fifth time – he kept squealing curses
and even told us how much he was worth – in a
moment of anger I smashed my coal shovel down
upon the back of the miser's skull. He fell to the
floor groaning. I kicked him three or four times
but Eddie restrained me and persuaded me against
finishing him off there and then, for while
Clanthorpe yet lived we might still be able to
discover where his fortune was hid!

'We could delay no longer for we were due back
at the sheds by half-past three – so we trussed the
old man up and put a corn-bag over his head, then
filled the remaining sack with all the plate we could
find and made our way back to the engine. The
fog was thick and concealed our every movement.
We hauled the corn bag and the old gentleman
over the garden wall, although no sooner had we
bundled him on to the footplate of the engine than
he expired, and with him any chance of our

discovering his fortune! Jeb knew of a mile post hut some way along the line towards Herne Hill. We shunted the locomotive back'ards and once we got to the hut dealt with Clanthorpe's body there.'

The brothers were reluctant to disclose any details concerning the whereabouts of the meat and poultry millionaire's body, however that morning as dawn slowly rose above the metropolis Holmes directed that the ash pan from the fire-box of the tank engine should be examined by a railway employee, and there, amongst the smouldering clinker, was found a battered skull and a number of cremated bones.

Brown, in his zealous hunt for the body, had also discovered, quite by accident, a large metal chest buried in a shallow trench beneath the old lichen-stained sun-dial in the garden: the Clanthorpe fortune in fact! However, this discovery was of little solace to Jeb and Eddie Parsons. Both brothers were tried, found guilty, and exactly three months from the day that Albert Locke walked free of Pentonville were hung by the neck until dead and certified so by the surgeon in attendance.

As a less sombre postscript, I can report that Albert Locke and his family are now happily farming sheep in New Zealand. The chimney sweep abandoned his brushes for a pair of shears and is doing very well out of it!

7

The Alumaenum Society

In glancing over my notes for the year 1897, the untimely death and tragic circumstance surrounding one of Mrs Hudson's closest friends, Mrs Gloria Staplehurst, a woman of considerable warmth and charitable inclination, draws my mind back to that bleak and rain-swept evening in October when, with lamps lit early and a good blaze roaring in the grate, my colleague, Mister Sherlock Holmes, sat in our sanctum playing the most melancholy passages upon his violin. Mrs Hudson had that day received, from Mrs Staplehurst's solicitors, a letter written by the deceased and discovered among her belongings. It seems she had omitted to post it to her friend.

Here I shall take the liberty of mentioning a word, perhaps not readily familiar to the reader: 'Summerland'. To elaborate, this is a spiritualist term, descriptive perhaps of the blissful state awaiting those who have passed 'through the veil' and are reunited with their loved ones upon the 'other side'. They enjoy a pleasant rebirth, free from care and the many, sometimes unendurable, trials that beset upon human kind in general.

That said, for those of us still amongst the earth-bound and yet to attain such giddy heights, everyday life is an ordained thing and we must do our best to embrace it wholeheartedly. The sudden demise of her husband, a man whom she had always loved and admired, must have prompted Mrs Staplehurst to embrace the Summerland concept perhaps a little before time. For aconite is one of the most rapidly effective poisons known to science.

That last unsent letter to Mrs Hudson, written in a resolved and meticulously neat hand, shortly before Mrs Staplehurst took her own life, contained many references to spiritualism and her recent conversion to it. She suggested her friend should contact the 'Alumaenum Society' and become acquainted with the principles and teachings of its founder, Marja Stallo. Mrs Hudson had lost no time in showing the letter to Holmes.

My companion abandoned his violin and examined the letter closely.

'I recall Mrs Staplehurst on her death, bequeathed a great deal of her husband's personal fortune to the Society,' Holmes said, tossing the letter aside.

'Well,' said I, 'that is surely a matter of her own free choice and should be best left unquestioned.'

After dinner, I sat back in my arm-chair opposite my companion and lit a cigar.

Outside I could hear the swish of carriage wheels, charging through the puddles formed during a particularly heavy cloudburst that afternoon and spread across the road like Amazonian lakes.

'Hereditary,' Holmes murmured from behind his newspaper. 'The Earl of Monkton gone – well, his Will shall, no doubt, be bitterly contested by his surviving brother and become the subject of lengthy and drawn-out litigation! Halloa! What the devil?'

The obituary column in *The Times* had evidently yielded some further intrigue and I was about to pass comment when my companion folded the paper, underlined a small section in ink, and tossed it across to me.

'What do you make of that?' said he, striking a match and lighting his pipe.

I studied the obituary page carefully. There was a small advertisement, which read:

Rejoined. Reunited
Tell the good news. There is no death.

Sceptics belonging to all creeds, harken. The Alumaenum Society can prove beyond all shadow of a doubt that the Summerland truly exists and life begins anew upon the other side.

'How wonderful realising my dearest husband did not leave me after all and that we are to be reunited in the Summerland, whence we shall enjoy such a happy and industrious life together. I am forever indebted to the Alumanenum Society for their guidance and my only wish is that others should benefit likewise.'
LYDIA MARCHMOUNT, Hampstead.

'Tell the good news. There is no death. This I do daily. The Alumaenum Society has placed

me regularly in touch with my beloved wife who now resides in the Summerland. Oh, what joy and to think I shall soon be joining her and my arthritis healed.
MR ALBERT MARSH, Streatham.

Those recently bereaved wishing to seek further information should apply in writing to: THE ALUMAENUM SOCIETY, 121-23 Lordship Lane, East Dulwich.

The following morning, we took a train to Croydon to visit one of Holmes's clients, a gentleman concerned about the forgery of his signature upon certain legal documents. A fellow passenger, getting on at Crystal Palace, happened to mention in passing that his neighbour, Mister Tadworth, a week after becoming a member of the Alumaenum Society, was found hanged in the conservatory of his house in Anerley. The police were loath to investigate the matter further, suspicious circumstances being ruled out on account of a note, scribbled shortly before his death, mentioning among other things the word 'Summerland'. Was this a reference to Eastbourne or Clacton, our friend wanted to know?

This most portentous opportunity arising out of a mere chance conversation in a railway carriage prompted my colleague to pursue the matter further and at Norwood Junction we changed trains and headed down the line in the direction of East Dulwich.

The headquarters of the Alumaenum Society, far from being ostentatious, was, as it turned out, modestly situated above the parlour of a funeral directors along Lordship Lane, in a rather seedy part of Dulwich, but three minutes' walk away from the railway station.

Next door were the undertakers' stables and workshop, approached by a cobbled walk. I observed through the lighted window a carpenter busily assembling coffins.

We knocked at the door, entered, and Holmes paused to admire his craftsmanship.

'Good sturdy English oak!' my colleague remarked, thumping the lid of a coffin with the flat of his hand. 'See how perfectly the corners are planed.'

The young man blew a fresh pile of wood shavings on to the floor. 'This one shall eventually be encased in a soldered lead box scored with a diamond twill pattern and inscription! Can I be of service to either of you two gentlemen?'

Holmes closed his eyes for a moment, and leaning upon his cane, stroked the ridge of his nose and murmured, 'Tell the good news! There is no death!' He then repeated the aforementioned 'Americanism' in a hushed voice.

The effect of this prayer-like incantation was not altogether lost upon the carpenter, who to my surprise immediately put down his chisel and bowed his head reverently.

'This, I do daily,' whispered the other, by way of a response.

The young man, who until now had appeared a trifle wary in our presence, became for some reason extraordinarily cordial and shook my companion warmly by the hand.

123

'I had no idea you were members of the Society!'
He shook my hand also and I nodded politely.

'Would you think it, perhaps, presumptuous if I
might enquire after Marja Stallo?' asked Holmes.

'Good gracious, no!' The young man beamed
from ear to ear and, seized by a paroxysm of
religious fervour, clasped his hands together. 'Our
most beloved communicator and revered deity, Her
Highness, the Divine Communicator from Neptune,
is at this very instant presiding over a séance with
a Mister Cummings, who lost his spouse recently.
Our firm organised the funeral last week.'

'A Mister Cummings, you say? I thought I saw
a fellow with a surgical shoe earlier, about your
age, I should think, dragging one foot behind the
other.'

'Ah, Mister Cummings is a spritely old gentleman,
who wears gaiters, Sir, and certainly not a cripple
with a gammy foot. You must have got the wrong
man!'

'Perhaps!' mused my colleague, glancing up at
the wall clock. 'My, is that the time already? Well,
we must rush! No doubt we shall all meet again
in the Summerland, eh?' Holmes quipped, a trifle
too facetiously. The prevailing mood of comradeship
and good humour was all at once replaced by a
distinctly cool atmosphere.

'That sacred word should never be intoned out
loud or taken in vain,' the young man, whose serene
expression had become most severe, said at length.
'Remember our vows! You are aware I trust of Marja
Stallo's commandments, enshrined in Section one
hundred and sixty of our Society's rule book?'

'Of course, how lax of me!' Holmes admitted, indicating by a three-fold wave of his cane that we should beat a hasty retreat before the fellow lost his temper altogether.

'And, shall I remember you both to Her Majesty if I see her?' the young man called with some malevolence. 'Your names are by the way...?'

'Mister Handel and Mister Trimmins,' said I, doffing my hat and marching briskly out of the door.

The weather had worsened in the last half-hour. It had grown colder and the fog was so dense along Lordship Lane that I could barely see the houses opposite.

Some road-menders, evidently implementing the Macadam system, were melting solid bricks of tar in buckets over a coke brazier, the molten pitch occasionally bubbling over the rim. We lost no time in warming our frozen hands by it.

Before we had a chance to thaw out, my colleague pointed anxiously at a shadowy figure rapidly receding into the fog.

'Watson, an elderly gentleman in gaiters has just this minute stepped out of the funeral director's – that door must surely lead upstairs to the Society's offices. It is Cummings! Hurry, or we shall lose him!'

It was quite a strain keeping up with him and just before the clock tower we observed the old gentleman cross over the road and disappear into a building from whence he did not emerge for some time.

The brass plaque above the entrance porch read:

MAW, DICKENSON AND DIMPOLE LIMITED SOLICITORS AND COMMISSIONERS OF OATHS

'He plans to alter his will, or at least add a codicil, I fear,' remarked Holmes, studying the inscription. 'My dear Watson, the old fellow has been taken in by all this Summerland twaddle and I fear it will be the devil's own job to keep him out of mischief!'

We paused to browse in a shop window and, appearing suitably inconspicuous, kept our eyes firmly fixed upon the glass-front until the familiar figure of Cummings was once again in our sights and we set off again. However, our task was considerably hampered by the fog which had descended upon the city and made everything appear spectral and ill-defined.

We breathlessly pursued the old gentleman all the way to Camberwell Green. Thereafter, he summoned a four-wheeler at Walworth Road and we, likewise, managed to procure a cab and were soon in hot pursuit.

At Lambeth clock tower, he abandoned transport altogether and proceeded to charge along the High Street on foot. At Lambeth Bridge the fog was so dense that we lost sight of him altogether. However, there was always the regular tap of his heel echoing against the walkway to keep us on the scent. He was by now presumably somewhere mid-way across the bridge, but I could hear nothing save the sound of dripping water and the foamy wash of the tide, swirling around the arches beneath.

For a moment the fog parted and I was able to observe a figure clamber precariously along the ledge of the bridge.

'In heaven's name, Watson, he plans to jump in!' whispered Holmes, creeping stealthily up behind.

The old gentleman was perched on the ledge, dressed in his top hat and frock-coat and leaning on a good-sized cane.

'Mister Cummings, my name is Sherlock Holmes and I am a consulting detective. This, by the way, is my colleague, Doctor Watson. Could I possibly have a word?'

The old gentleman appeared completely taken aback by our intrusion into his thoughts. 'Good God! Who the devil are you? What is the meaning of this?' he demanded.

'I shall detain you no longer than is absolutely necessary, Mister Cummings. The facts are these: Mrs Staplehurst, a member of the Alumaenum Society, recently poisoned herself. Mister Tadworth, a fellow member, was found hanged at his house in Anerley! Why, in the final analysis, these persons like yourself have been taken unfair advantage of!'

'I have not the slightest idea what you are talking about!' he said indignantly, turning once more to face the murky depths of the Thames.

'Promises of life after death, a re-birth free from all bodily ills and mental aberrations! How much of your personal fortune did you bequeath to the Society for the privilege of being duped?'

'Away with you, Sir!' he shouted, striking his stick upon the ledge with some petulance.

'Tell the good news! There is no death! That is

her slogan. Do you know of whom I speak, Mister Cummings?'

'Yes, yes, you refer to the Society's founder, Marja Stallo, and I can say that her *modus operandi* are perfectly genuine. Upon the death of my own physical body, after firstly disposing of, at least, seventy per cent of my income and property to the Society, she promises to use her considerable influence to direct my astral being to a spirit world far more fair-minded and wonderful than ours, called the Summerland. That dear and compassionate woman is to reunite me with my wife and my firm resolve shall not be shaken one jot by your malicious bickerings, Mister Holmes!'

'Come, man!' my friend interceded. 'The woman is a fraudulent trickster, her Society a sham!'

'I must beg to differ, Sir. She is a medium of the highest repute!'

With these final words of defiance the old gentleman shut his eyes and prepared to take the plunge. However, my friend must have installed a niggling doubt in the old fellow's mind for he hovered on the brink of suicide for a moment or two and then withdrew altogether.

'I cannot do it!' he sighed.

'Capital! I perceive you are not entirely bereft of sanity after all, Mister Cummings! Come down from that great height and stop acting like a madman!'

'You said Marja Stallo is a fraud?' Cummings remarked as we assisted him down from the bridge.

'I did. Meanwhile, sip this brandy, you look frozen!'

'Perhaps I have been a trifle over-zealous, although

I confess I never once thought to question the Society's motives. But, tell me this, Mister Holmes, a sensitive is, by tradition, a psychic: a person who is able to contact the spirit world and communicate with those beyond the grave. Pray, why are you such a sceptic? Are not such things truly possible?'

'Table rappers, trumpets and rattling castanets are not really my forte, Mister Cummings, however, the murky and ill-defined depths of the criminal mind are much more to my personal taste and I think that, perhaps, with your assistance I will implement a little scheme which shall prove beyond a shadow of doubt that this Society and, in particular, its founder are none other than a gang of cold-hearted opportunists, whose evil aspirations are conveniently disguised under the cloak of spiritualism. However, we must firstly make it appear that you jumped off Lambeth Bridge. A prominent article placed in all the morning editions might help: "Elderly gentleman Cummings, drowned in Thames. Body found floating towards Greenwich by the River Police. No foul play suspected."

'Something like that! Meanwhile, I suggest you return with myself and Doctor Watson here to our cosy little rooms in Baker Street and enjoy a good supper prepared by our esteemed housekeeper, Mrs Hudson. I daresay you can have a hot bath and take the couch for the night. Tomorrow morning we shall endeavour to dissolve the Alumaenum Society once and for all!'

The next morning, as our cab rattled along the foggy London streets towards Dulwich, I sat beside a widow in deepest mourning, who wore a black bonnet and dress. Her stern and aristocratic features were wholly concealed by a gauze veil, and yet her sombre aspect was marred slightly by the presence of an old briar pipe, the smoke of which filled our carriage with the reek of the strongest shag tobacco.

'My dear Watson,' proclaimed the widow, whose pseudonym was, incidentally, Mrs Hope, 'the Society shall have received my wire by now embossed in a suitable black surround, conveying in the most eloquent terms my desire to communicate with the dead, in particular, my dear, departed husband, Charles. I quoted that trashy phrase, "Tell the good news! There is no death!", and begged Marja Stallo to show me how to communicate with those on the other side. Of course, I also happened to mention in passing that my late husband was a director on the board of the largest banking firm in the country!'

'I cannot imagine how the Society should be able to resist such pickings!' I answered, with some amusement.

'I made it perfectly clear that I could only spare an hour or two and that the séance should take place at eleven o'clock, this morning. A final proviso insisted that my brother, Antony, should be present at the séance to support me in my hour of grief.'

'Naturally!'

'We have just passed East Dulwich station and shall soon be at the Society's offices!'

* * *

'You have heard mention of Mister D.D. Hume, I trust?'

'I believe not,' said the widow.

'A medium of rare and considerable powers, my dear Mrs Hope. D.D. Hume has performed before royalty and leaders of nations,' said the Secretary of the Society, Mr Bellows, leading us up a flight of stairs. 'But, Marja Stallo is even greater than he.'

We were shown into a back room overlooking the funeral director's cobbled yard and stables. The windows were tinged with dirt from the atmosphere and the chintzes were half-drawn.

A sea-coal fire glowed comfortably enough in the grate, although outside the immediate orbit of the fire I was struck by the icy chill of the place. A red lamp shone from the centre of the ceiling, shedding a somewhat bleak light upon the polished surface of a round mahogany table beneath. There was little furniture in evidence, save for an upright piano and several hard-backed chairs.

A rotund, jolly-looking woman, sporting a patch over one eye and a top hat, mantled in voluminous bright and gaily-coloured Chinese silks, sat motionless on an elderly wicker chair, puffing away on a cheroot.

'Ah, Mrs Hope, how good of you to visit our offices! And this is Antony, I take it? Do sit down, Sir, mere formalities are a drudge with me. Do either of you take herbal tea? The colour of your brother's aura gives me cause for grave concern, Mrs Hope. Might I suggest a suitable prophylactic? Mustard oil, else, spoonwort, perhaps?'

131

We drank our herbal tea, the flavour of which I personally detested, in silence. I confess this Grand Dame of the Alumaenum Society seemed, upon first impressions at least, neither sinister nor her personality particularly alarming. On the contrary, her cheerful manner and eccentric dress sense only added to the enjoyment of the occasion and, yet, I had not the slightest doubt that a woman of such poise and self-possession was capable of employing immense cunning to obtain her own wicked ends.

'Now, if I might have your attention?'

The sensitive waved her chubby ring-bedecked hand above a circle of cards laid out before us, each card bearing a different letter of the alphabet.

'The hub of my communication,' she confided.

'And, I hear that you can effect levitation on occasions?' remarked my companion, placing his cup and saucer aside.

'Up to the ceiling, my dear.'

The medium adjusted her eye-patch and gazed at her own reflection in the oval mirror above the mantelpiece.

'I propose to take you both upon a voyage of discovery.'

'A voyage?' said I.

'The Summerland,' she sighed. 'Why, Antony, I shall soon let your sister into a little secret. Remember, life is but a fleeting thing, but death?' She smiled. 'You shall soon be reunited with your beloved husband. Hush! I can sense a handsome gentleman possessed of great dignity and resolve, materialising in the spiritual ethers.'

'I recognise to whom you refer, Madam,' answered

Holmes. 'Oh, there is so little left for me in this world since the passing of my dear husband.'

'Material things – tut, tut – we are apt to place far too much importance upon capital, railway shares, government bonds and such-like, Mrs Hope,' she answered, patting the widow's hand affectionately.

'Oh, I should gladly part with my entire fortune if I could but see my dear husband again.'

'A hymn!' Marja Stallo cried, triumphantly. 'A hymn, Mr Bellows, and be quick! The shadows are gathering and I can feel the presence of someone recently departed in the room!'

Accompanied on the piano, we burst into a terrible off-key rendition of 'All Creatures Great and Small'. I did not think the Secretary's playing up to much. He thumped the keys violently and worked the pedal with a clumsy foot!

At last, the hymn ended. Bellows rose from his stool and departed. Thereafter, we linked hands and mumbled a short prayer.

A glass-covered clock upon the mantelpiece chimed the half-hour in a pretty and melodious sequence of notes and barely had we touched our finger-tips upon the surface of the upturned glass than Holmes, quite unexpectedly, flung his arms in the air, setting all the cards a-flutter, and fell back in his chair, rolling his eyes deliriously. He made quite a show of it but the queerest thing was the brilliant blue flash that lit up the darkened room shortly before this calculated outburst.

Moaning in a high-pitched soprano voice and, thereafter, alternating to a deep basso, my colleague, alias the widow Mrs Hope, rocked back and forth upon the legs of her chair and proceeded to give Marja Stallo a hard time of it.

'Imposter!' he murmured, before a dough-like substance oozed from his mouth – running profusely down the front of his dress.

The woman looked aghast, unable to believe her eyes!

'Adopting the guise of a spiritualist society, you and your crew have lined each other's pockets with fool's gold. The Alumaenum Society is but a sham and thee a charlatan! Beware, I say, lest you die and be condemned to drift for aeons in the fog-bound lower astrals!'

The sensitive wailed piteously. However, her breakdown was not solely because of Holmes's antics but rather something else far more fiendish still. I turned round to witness a ghostly face peering in through the window.

'A phantasm!' she shrieked, pointing at the chintzes with a trembling finger. ''Tis old man Cummings risen from, the dead! –Dear Lord, I cannot bear to look! His head is covered with slime and weeds from the river-bed! Please!' Her top-hat tumbled to the floor as she put her head in her hands and wept.

'Spirit, I admit I am guilty upon all charges!' she exclaimed. 'I have dishonestly fleeced the wills of the bereaved and committed falsehoods too numerous to mention. The worst of these deceptions being the promise that upon death, under my spiritual tutelage, I should guide the astral bodies of my clients to meet with their loved ones in the hereafter!'

My companion sprang from his chair, discarded his funerary attire and promptly pointed a revolver at Bellows, who had just burst into the room.

'Quite still, if you please! My name is Sherlock Holmes and I am a consulting detective,' he said with a determined look. 'I should keep your ground if I were you, else you might tempt me to brush my finger against this delicate, if rather lightly sprung mechanism. Ha! Quite singular and effective what a stepladder and a little theatrical grease can do, eh, Watson! A mixture of gun-powder and phosphorous were responsible for the brilliant explosion of light earlier, by the way, and I have since discovered baker's dough compounded with a little tea, well masticated for a few minutes, provides a first-rate stimulation of ectoplasm!'

'I am rumbled!' cried the medium, woefully, 'and I had hoped to one day own a fine mansion in Belgravia and a fashionable sea-front house in Brighton. Oh, my carriage, Georgian residence in Northumberland Avenue and my long and leisurely rides along the promenade, accompanied by my servants, a page boy or three, are all in ruins!'

'Rumbled, indeed,' agreed Holmes, putting aside his revolver and tossing his widow's hat and veil across the room. 'Now Madam, might I suggest the Alumaenum Society be hereby dissolved? And, oh yes, you and your Secretary friend might like to take a trip abroad to visit some foreign parts! Do I make myself plain?'

'Perfectly,' the medium sobbed; a more pathetic individual it would be hard to imagine.

'There's the making of a good newspaper article

in this and, from what I've heard, so far, enough evidence to put you in Holloway for a lengthy stretch. Start up again at your peril! Ah, my dear Mister Cummings, I trust you have not been too incommoded? Your performance was highly entertaining!'

'And, I am glad you appreciated it, Sir,' said he, coming into the room and wiping away at his face with a handkerchief. 'Although, the height of the ladder did not entirely agree with my digestive organs!'

'Well, well, a little fresh air, at least!' answered Holmes, curtly. 'One glimpse of your character study of a drowned man was more than enough to exact a confession, and now, my dear Watson, a little lunch at Marcini's, followed by a concert of Beethoven at Covent Garden. Perhaps, Mister Cummings, you would care to join us upon our little musical foray?'

'I should be delighted, Sir!' the old gentleman replied.

'Good-day, Madam,' said Holmes finally, with a slight bow. 'Start up again at your peril: remember what I have said! The boat train to Newhaven runs from Victoria on the hour, by the way. I trust you will not be too late to catch it!'

8

The Streatham Cemetery Scandal

I am about to summarise certain events which took place in the Michaelmas of '93, the nature of which might provide the reader with some idea of the considerable deductive powers of my friend, Sherlock Holmes. For even when faced by the most sensitive and frankly disturbing melodrama of the day, he could keep a clear head where others become befuddled, observe the most trifling of details, otherwise neglected, and with a sureness and rapidity none could match, bring a case to a successful conclusion because of it.

One bitterly cold morning in December, I ventured out into the sleet and visited Bradley's, the tobacconist. Upon my return to our little habitation in Baker Street, I encountered – albeit fleetingly – a personage known to me from the murky past before ever I visited Afghanistan, else fell foul of a Jezail bullet at the fatal Battle of Maiwand.

'Ha, Watson,' said my colleague, huddled in his dressing gown and tuning and re-tuning his violin. 'Did you perchance observe that singular fellow upon the stairs, earlier?'

'Professor Sir James Wilkes,' said I, rubbing my

frozen hands in front of the fire. 'I remember Wilkes from my time spent at the University of London. His lectures were always monotonous! He belongs to the old school of dissectionists. What did he have to say, anyhow?'

'He came to consult me professionally. The popular Fleet Street press are, he believes, about to launch a vindictive and slanderous campaign against his hospital, and teaching hospitals in general!'

'The resurrectionists!'

'Just so,' replied my colleague, staring out of the window at the dense traffic rattling along the snow-covered thoroughfare beneath.

'"The London", quite wrongly, he intimated, is named as being the main beneficiary!'

A somewhat guilty flush surfaced upon my cheeks, as I remembered my own carefree days spent in the dissection room.

Holmes smiled. 'A specimen has its value!'

'Oh, quite so, my dear Holmes, but that said there exist perfectly legal and proper means of obtaining them. This recent spate of body-snatching in South London has not gone down well with the public!'

'And the fact that there were minors involved!'

'Doubly awful,' I conceded.

'Yet, the fact that Doctor Rudyard Firebrace was found murdered, stabbed to death in the drawing room of his mews house in Mortimer Place, Knightsbridge, gets hardly a mention in the morning editions,' said my companion with a sigh, producing a snatch of Mendelssohn on his violin.

'Doctor Rudyard Firebrace? Didn't he have something to do with diamonds?' I asked.

'Yes, he stole them, Watson! Mostly on the Continent in France and Italy. Ah, is that the doorbell I hear?'

Not long afterwards Inspector Lestrade, looking rather ragged and rumpled, entered our airy sitting room.

'The compliments of the season,' he said with the dreariest of smiles.

'I perceive by your wind-blown complexion and the state of your shoes that you have been stood about on some exposed place. There exists a singular streak along the length of your heavy, broadcloth coat, perhaps, masonry dust, and I observe your right middle fingers are smeared with lamp oil. We can, therefore, safely assume that you were called out in the early hours of the morning.'

'Norwood Cemetery, Mister Holmes!'

'So, the problem escalates,' said I.

'I am afraid that is the case, Doctor Watson. Another pauper's grave defiled and, yet, this time the child's body was left behind. Perhaps, the resurrection-men were interrupted while performing their grisly task!'

'The corpse was abandoned, you say?' said my colleague.

'That's about the run of it!'

'Well, I hope they shall be caught soon!' I commented, taking up a cigar from the coal scuttle and lighting it.

'Oh, I agree entirely, Doctor Watson,' answered Lestrade, with a baffled look. 'Perhaps, Mister Holmes and yourself would be good enough to accompany me back to the cemetery, for I have drawn a complete blank so far and should be glad of some assistance.'

'We should be delighted, Inspector!' said Holmes, flinging aside his purple dressing gown. 'Let us hope the weather does not turn colder. Each fresh fall of snow shall hamper our investigation considerably. Incidentally, does the name Rudyard Firebrace mean anything to you?'

'The doctor was murdered in mysterious circumstances and we have, so far, been unable to apprehend the persons responsible for the crime.'

'Quite!' answered Holmes, replacing his violin in its case. 'Well, I have seen worse weather, I suppose, although this morning it is our misfortune to be out in it. Come, my dear Watson, wrap up well and let's get going!'

We arrived at Norwood Cemetery a little after eleven. A horse had slipped upon the hill and a hansom overturned. Mercifully, neither the horse nor its owner were injured, although there was a heated argument going on between the cabman and a pedestrian.

Our four-wheeler trundled sedately past the lodge gates and proceeded along a sweeping, shingle drive, hemmed in by multitudinous rows of headstones and tombs until we reached a place on higher ground more barren and exposed than the rest.

There, overlooking Norwood Hill and the suburbs was a grassy plot bordered by trees and dotted about with tiny lozenge-shaped markers, each cast in iron and bearing a number. On the far side beyond the desecrated grave was the piteous sight of a roughly-made coffin, the metal hinges of the lid much bent about and twisted out of true.

'The Latin numerals upon each marker presumably indicate how recently the paupers were buried?' remarked Holmes, striding ahead.

'That is correct, Mister Holmes!' replied Lestrade, shouting after him and blowing out a good deal of air. 'The resurrection-men have chosen in every case the graves of children who have died from the recent fever epidemic in the workhouses.'

Holmes squatted upon his haunches and poked the clay, thereabouts, with his long thin cane. Although it was not snowing, the bitterly cold wind coming off the hill blew fiercely against our faces. 'No sign of a barrow, else a dog-cart, there are no wheel ruts, although the hard frost we had this morning has preserved a nice foot-print or two! Halloa! A gentleman, I see!'

'A gentleman! And, how on earth do you deduce that, Holmes?' said I.

'My dear Watson, I have discovered the remains of a half-smoked Havana cigar of the finest quality and a singular foot-print belonging to a dainty gentleman's shoe, possibly a size seven, purchased from Lobbs in Regent Street. He appears to have stood in one place for most of the time.'

'Remarkable!'

'The other person – for there were two of them – whom I should say did the lion's share of the work, was stockily built and a trifle bow-legged. However, this is mere conjecture! Come, Watson, let us fly to Simpsons! Once planted in more congenial surroundings, we can sample some of their excellent roast beef, enjoy a glass of burgundy and mull over the problem. Nothing more can be done for the present, Inspector! I shall report back to you by wire shortly.'

What greater contrast then after a good lunch at Simpsons, the congenial atmosphere of St James Hall and the stirring music of Beethoven's violin concerto. Holmes sat in the stalls, finger-tips placed together, with his eyes shut and a serene smile upon his lips, for the first movement certainly, but, then quite unexpectedly, he tapped my shoulder and indicated we should leave – at once!

'Watson,' he said, in barely a whisper, 'we must hasten to Baker Street. Here, take your hat and scarf – never mind the stares – look sharp towards the foyer!'

My companion's impulsive nature, wedded to a fierce and energetic drive to get things done, had long ago ceased to surprise me. Once outside, we hastily summoned a cab to take us back to Baker Street. There, in more congenial surroundings, Holmes seized his black clay from the rack upon the mantelpiece, fell back into his armchair, and smoked for a full quarter hour.

'Do you, perchance, recall the Bank of Jerrards & Co. in Knightsbridge was robbed recently, Watson?' said he, at length, peering at me languidly through the thick fug of noxious tobacco fumes.

'Yes, the safety deposit boxes were rifled!' I answered, relighting my cigar.

'They contained a quantity of diamonds lodged there by De Beers to the tune of some eighty thousand pounds.'

'Quite, and despite a large reward offered by the company, the perpetrators have still to be apprehended!'

'The criminals were a masterly gang. And, by the considerable pertinacity and flair of the operation, I should say a foreign one. The Cambierré Brothers – Antoine and Jean Claude, for instance!'

'The Bank d'Paris was robbed last January and the Frenchmen were linked with that crime, also,' said I, leaning back in my chair and gazing at the smoke-filled ceiling.

'And, someone else, I believe?'

'Good Lord, Holmes! Doctor Rudyard Firebrace, the murdered man you mentioned earlier!'

'Precisely, Watson! The good doctor owns a mews house in Knightsbridge and the bank of Jerrards & Co. is only a short distance away, round the corner from Harrods, in fact. Let us suppose the entire operation was master-minded from there. After the robbery, why, the Frenchmen would surely have taken the boat train to Dover and, thence, a steam packet for Europe. However, if a complication of sorts arose and these gentlemen should be unavoidably detained in this country?'

'Now I catch your drift, Holmes. You believe the doctor was, for whatever reason, murdered because of this complication?'

'Bravo, dear boy!' Holmes put his pipe aside and shut his eyes for a moment.

'And where does that lead us?' I parried, barely able to contain my excitement.

'To the workhouse!'

Before I could reply, Holmes sprang from his

chair and drew back the blinds a little to watch the flakes of snow swirling about outside the window, gathering in great heaps upon either side of the lintels. Thus began our expedition to the South London workhouses. For all the diplomacy of my colleague, Sherlock Holmes, his pertinent questions were, for the most part, greeted with lethargic indifference, else downright insolence.

The Masters in charge of these seedy establishments were for the most part a race of Bohemians, closeted behind workhouse gates, who guarded their squalid wards jealously. Our tour finally ended at Streatham workhouse. We were confronted on the porch steps by the Master, a bow-legged old ruffian, named Lubbock, dressed in a ragged frock-coat, scarf and mittens to fend off the cold, whose gaunt features appeared all the more ghastly and phantasmal under the dull vacillating light from the gas jet above.

The dirty fellow scratched his beard and indicated with a shivering hand to his booth, just beyond the entrance.

'Are ye the Inspectors come about the cracked windas in the imbeciles ward or the drains?'

Holmes promptly retrieved a shiny sovereign and waved it in front of the old derelict's face.

'We require a little information!'

Lubbock became suddenly animated and snatched the coin.

'Do you, perhaps, recall a gentleman calling here recently, asking after one of the children in your care?'

'No Sur, I do not! Only the undertaker and our

regular practitioner, Doctor Symes! There has been a tiresome outbreak of cholera fever. Some blame the drains, but I prefer to put it down to ungodliness – that, and not enough bone-grinding, else oakum pickin! The Scriptures tell us that idleness brings death to them who does not perform an honest day's work!'

This detestable statement from one who probably did nothing more industrious than raise a jug of gin to his lips brought our interview to a close. However, we were about to turn on our heels when Lubbock seized my companion's sleeve and whispered:

'Though there was an old tar from the East India I shared a pipe with a week ago!'

'What was the nature of his visit?' asked Holmes, slinging his scarf over his shoulder and stamping his feet upon the porch steps, for the weather was severe and the temperature must have surely dropped another notch or two below zero.

'Well, Sur, the old fella was a cripple what walked with a crutch – a great woolly shock of fiery red hair and beard to match! 'E mentioned a boy o' mine called Tom – been 'ere since a babe like.'

'And, did you allow this old tar to see the boy?'

'The child was not long for this world, Sur, and I did not – but he gave me a dirty parcel to give him all the same. Now, let me examine the register …'

We waited there upon the steps for what seemed like an eternity, while short-sighted Lubbock thumbed through the grubby, yellowish pages of his book.

'A pair o' breeches! That's what he told me the parcel contained,' the fellow said at length.

'And what became of this parcel?'

'It were put along with a cheap watch that never worked proper but the lad was regular fond of, and some religious tracts that 'e hated above all else, inside of the coffin, Sur, 'tis the custom.'

'Inside the boy's coffin, you say. And when did the funeral take place? Come on man, hurry!'

'Tom died yesterday and was buried at state expense this afternoon at Streatham Cemetery. The hearse was shabby and there were few flowers. Mister Dobson, the undertaker, usually takes care of...'

'Capital! Capital!' Holmes interrupted Lubbock's funerary monologue and, with a wave of his hat, said cheerily, 'May I and my colleague, Doctor Watson, here be the first to offer you the compliments of the season! Good-day!'

'Well,' said I, 'we are evidently no nearer to discovering the movements of this fellow, Doctor Firebrace! He did not visit the Streatham workhouse at any rate!'

'On the contrary, my dear Watson,' said my colleague, lighting a cigarette. 'Do you recall mention of the cripple with the woolly shock of fiery-red hair?'

'The old tar from the East India, you mean?'

'A wig!'

'The fellow was wearing a wig!' I ejaculated.

'I am certain the aforementioned sailor was none other than Doctor Rudyard Firebrace. In fact, I am convinced upon the point. The crutch is, as you

146

know, a favourite ruse of my own, employed from time to time whenever the need arises!'

After supper, my colleague, having earlier wired Inspector Lestrade at Scotland Yard, proposed that we visit Streatham Cemetery to keep a constant vigil over the pauper's plot where the child had been buried.

Later, adequately concealed behind the vast circumference of banked-up hedgerow trees overlooking the vicinity of the plot, we sat shivering in our coats like a group of Afghan tribesmen, with scarves drawn tightly over our faces, staving off the wind which cut relentlessly across the cemetery.

At nine o'clock, Lestrade observed the gleam of an oil lantern bobbing up and down behind some trees. Thereafter, two fellows brazenly stepped out from the darkness and, showing not the slightest propriety, else respect for the dead, trudged across the many graves thereabouts.

'*Que le temps anglais est miserable et sale!*' said one of them.

'*Mais, çela va sans dire!*' answered the other.

The tallest, an aristocratic gentleman of fine poise, dressed impeccably in frock-coat, top hat and spats, leaned back against the fence and, taking out a leather cigar case, watched his more burly companion, an imposing Atlas of a figure, throw down his kit-bag and start digging with a spade.

'About there,' said he, with some amusement, lighting a cigar and throwing away the match.

'I know where to dig!' the other cursed, uprooting and tossing aside an iron marker.

147

'The ground is hard!' the gentleman resurrectionist remarked, occasionally glancing at his gold repeater between puffs on his cigar.

'*Pourtant, ce n'est pas aussi dur qu'un diamant, hein!*' commented the other wryly, wiping his massive bull-like neck with a cravat.

Soon the pauper's grave had been uncovered and by the dull thud of the spade I perceived that the coffin had been struck and this scurrilous enterprise was nearing its close.

Upon a wave of Holmes's long cane, we dashed across the muddy ground to confront the villains.

'*Mon dieu!*' The gentleman resurrectionist unbuttoned his frock-coat and retrieved a miniature gambler's pistol.

'Hum, a Derringer, I see!' said Holmes, knocking the weapon from the Frenchman's hand with a deft strike of his cane upon the fellow's knuckles. 'The night is a trifle chilly, I suggest you keep your service revolver firmly clasped against that burly fellow's head, Watson!'

The tall gentleman adopted a haughty and indolent posture. 'I am a citizen of the Republique, a member of the French nobility, and demand diplomatic immunity!' He then tried another tack. 'My dear Sir, forgive me, I was merely passing and noticed a light in the cemetery. I came upon this ruffian of a fellow going about his despicable business of *vol des tombes*! I was, of course, like every dutiful citizen about to … '

'Enough!' Lestrade said sternly, applying the cuffs.

'And, if I might say so, what a grievous slant against your brother, Jean Claude, who will, no doubt, be grateful for your support under such trying circumstances!' joked Holmes. 'Perhaps Inspector Lestrade here might offer you both warm lodgings for the night?'

'You jest at the expense of a gentleman of honour!' the Frenchman exclaimed, delivering his final broadside, with little effect!

'My dear Watson, may I introduce the Cambierré Brothers, one-time circus trapeze artists, now, amongst the most accomplished diamond thieves in the entire European hemisphere! *Voila!* The French Bureau should be interested to hear about their most recent *leurs vacances courts* abroad I think!'

By the time we returned to our diggings, it was snowing heavily. While my colleague slouched in his big arm-chair before the fire, smoking his old briar and pasting some obituary notices into one of his voluminous scrap books, I poured us a whisky and soda.

'Presuming the parcel inside the coffin does contain the missing De Beers' diamonds, Holmes, I still cannot fathom for the life of me why Rudyard Firebrace chose to conceal the diamonds in such a reckless and irrational fashion.'

'Oh, it was not random, Watson. The doctor was a very clever man and knew precisely what he was doing!'

'A cold-hearted scoundrel!' said I.

'Not so cold-hearted as you might think. Let us suppose Firebrace was genuinely enquiring after the boy. Now, we must discover the real motive behind the visit: to elicit a hiding place for the gems, or to give the child something? A gift, perhaps, to make amends for the past and ease a father's wretched conscience? A gift that would some day help transform his son from being a pauper living at state expense to one of the richest men in Europe?'

'Good Lord, an illegitimate heir, Holmes!'

'I believe that to be the case, Watson. An illicit union took place. The child was abandoned by its poor mother and left to the dreary auspices of the workhouse. Many years must have elapsed before Firebrace, now a wealthy widower, without issue, tracked him down and learnt of the child's fate. Alas, tragedy struck, for his son was already dying from cholera when he visited the workhouse in the guise of the bewigged, crippled tar from the East India, but even this did not deter him from his purpose, for, no doubt, heart-broken, he handed the packet into the workhouse just the same. I believe Rudyard Firebrace, desperate to make amends for the past: after the Knightsbridge bank robbery decided to keep the entire haul of diamonds for himself. A treacherous business! The Cambierré brothers are a shrewd and murderous pair of fellows to swindle, Watson. They would quickly realise who stole their share of the diamonds from under their very noses and must have extorted a confession from Firebrace before murdering him. Perhaps, under the duress, he mentioned the workhouse and the death of his illegitimate son, but, more importantly, the custom of possessions of the deceased being placed inside the coffin, along with the corpse! However,' my friend wagged his long finger, 'he was obviously not specific and Antoine and Jean Claude were left with a considerably weighty conundrum!'

'And the diamonds are, at present, sealed within the child's coffin!'

'And, of course, Inspector Lestrade shall need the coroner's permission to open it!'

Our conversation was interrupted by the loud clang of the doorbell downstairs. Instantly, a brass band started up and a festive carol, conducted at a brisk military tempo, and accompanied by a bevy of enthusiastic voices, echoed along the street.

Holmes sprang from his chair and snatched his violin. He drew back the blinds and, despite the cold weather, half-opened the window.

'Dig deep into your pockets, my dear Watson!'

'Carol singers!' said I, getting up to join him.

'And, I think I shall accompany them on my violin. Tara, tara! Good Christian men rejoice with heart and ... come, Watson, you're an excellent baritone! Come over here by the window, there's a good fellow! Tara, tara!'

9

The Black Brougham

The season of goodwill was upon us, I and Mr
Sherlock Holmes caught in a seething mass of
humanity, a crowd of determined pedestrians intent
on jostling their way through the doors of a palatial
department store. We somehow managed to escape
the clamour and, approaching Marble Arch, the
carriage traffic and drays much in evidence, were
surprised to see our friend Ralph Cosworth alight
from a crowded omnibus. He was brandishing a
stout walking stick, and well wrapped up against
the sleet and snow in a winter overcoat and bowler
hat. Crossing Oxford Street, he waved at us.

'Mr Holmes, Doctor Watson, a pleasure to see
you. I am by way of diversion doing a little window
shopping before visiting my bank manager.'

Ralph had recently lost his father, and was expected
to inherit a considerable sum.

'The will's been read,' said I, presuming it had, for
the last time we spoke at a concert of Scarlatti at the
Wigmore Hall, a positive outcome seemed assured.

'Oh, the will was read ages ago,' said he, a trifle
petulantly, giving me a fierce stare.

'And the Cosworth fortune?' asked Holmes,

clapping his pigskin gloves together to fend off the worst of the cold, for Oxford Street was under invasion from an easterly Siberian wind, leaving the West End of London in the grip of Arctic temperatures.

'Alas, gentlemen, I am in a state of penury. Bank loans and investment in new machinery shortly before my father's death have left the firm in debt. My creditors appear at every turn – soon my house shall have to be sold and my family put out on the streets. The annual turkey dinner for all employees and their families held at the Stag and Hounds has been cancelled for the first time since the business was established.'

'But, the company under your stewardship continues to turn out Cosworth wrought-iron gates and garden furniture, and railings for public parks.'

'There has been a downturn and we are facing competition from a Birmingham metalworker – the last substantial order was in September for railings for the Crystal Palace Parade.'

'But what's happened to all the money?' said I, flabbergasted at our friend's sudden fall from grace.

'My father was always cagey in his financial dealings, but I confess I was utterly dumbfounded when the will was read out and I discovered I had been left no money whatsoever – instead I had been bequeathed a black brougham, not worth a jot, of the type preferred by undertakers for use as a mourning coach.'

I laughed heartily but Holmes hushed me up by means of digging me in the ribs for he understood Cosworth was sorely perplexed on the point.

'I apologise,' said I, wiping away a tear. 'I shouldn't take this reading of wills so lightly, but tell me,

Ralph, your father was worth a fortune. Surely there is something in the pot for you.'

'I believe the whole lot went to some missionary charity for waifs and strays in Africa. My father was always reticent, or at least buttoned up when it came to the importance of inheritance, but during his final illness – the last week or two of his life – his mind became unhinged. He who was always steadfast and honest became secretive and canny, especially about money. He had always been such a generous fellow but he fell into penny-pinching and miserly ways. It was sad for Megan and the children to witness, but there we are.'

'And the black brougham?'

'Oh Lord, Mr Holmes – straight from a funeral firm – its coachwork is black, worn-out purple plush seats, nickel coach lamps. I detest the thing and can't wait to be rid of it. How many cemeteries it's visited I dare not think.'

'And your London works is Shoreditch way, isn't it?'

'Yes, Mr Holmes, all our iron railings and garden furniture is made there.'

'And where is the black brougham at present?'

'It resides at the Shoreditch works, parked in the cobbled yard next to a redundant boiler, awaiting the rag and bone man. If only I had inherited this money as originally intended my firm would have easily survived the downturn and the new machinery adapted to produce a broader range. As it is, I am now facing bankruptcy and ruin.'

I should mention that exposure to the biting wind driving down Oxford Street had left my face numb and rigid like a stone-cold block of marble. I thus suggested we should continue our conversation in a warmer, more sheltered situation, and enjoy a good lunch at a convenient diner. However, poor Cosworth declined, bid us good day and headed off towards the Holborn end, instantly lost to the milling crowds. It was sad to see such a normally affable individual, full of bonhomie, broken in this way. The blow to his finances must have been doubly awful due to it being Christmas week.

* * *

Over lunch at a nearby diner, my companion ate little and was obviously distracted. I enjoyed my lamb cutlets while he left his plate mostly untouched. Smoking our pipes at the conclusion of our meal he suggested a journey across London to Shoreditch might be in order.

'Oh that black brougham,' said I. 'Are you keen on purchasing the old carriage?'

My friend smiled wanly at my good-natured jibe, puffing on his briar pipe and frowning the more intently.

'You know, Watson, this matter of the will bothers me. All the old man's wealth apparently gone to charity. Was Cosworth Senior coerced in some way to alter the original, else include a codicil?'

'I am frankly appalled at the possibility of Ralph Cosworth and his family being cast out onto the streets. The firm he has worked so hard to build up over the years going to the dogs,' said I bluntly.

'Dear me, it's a practical solution we seek, Watson, not to write the poor fellow's obituary. Let us summon a cab and make haste for Cosworth's factory. My, I must call in at the tobacconists for I am running low on cigarettes.'

By the time we reached the Shoreditch works it was sleeting hard. Lamps had been lit inside the factory and we were greeted by a hooter summoning a tea break, yet all the while we were there the grinding and milling of metal and the forging of iron railings did not abate.

Beyond the gates lay the cobbled yard, the grim Leviathan of the black brougham parked just as Ralph had described, the hood covered in a thin layer of settling sleet. I shuddered as I recalled Cosworth's gloomy words about its visits to so many cemeteries. I guessed the brougham was second- or even third-hand.

Holmes, ignoring the wet sleet, ventured to walk round it a couple of times. He tapped the coachwork with his cane, looked inside, scowling at the jaded upholstery and the blinds partly drawn. He stooped a little.

'No serial number or carriage-builder's plate,' he murmured. He stepped back and waved me over. 'Watson,' said he. 'What strikes you as singularly odd about the appearance of the old brougham?'

I got down on my haunches and examined the carriage.

'You are aware of some minor discrepancy,' said he, pursing his lips.

'On the contrary, Holmes. I am aware of a major discrepancy,' said I, 'for the wheels look far too large and cumbersome for the carriage.'

'Bravo, Watson, an excellent point. You will observe

the rims and spokes are freshly painted with tradesman's black gloss. They appear to be brand-new additions. The coachwork on the other hand shows signs of wear and tear.'

* * *

The following morning Holmes was reading *The Telegraph*, sat in his favourite armchair, his long legs stretched in front of the fire.

Returning from Shoreditch we had stopped off at Marylebone Public Library and my companion borrowed a weighty tome, a reference work on carriage vehicles. Back at our diggings, over a whisky and soda, with the gas jets well turned up, we discovered on page 151 a diagram, a construction plan relating to the old brougham presently berthed in Ralph's works yard. Built by the coach-building firm of Locketts, this type of carriage was indeed popular with the undertaking fraternity, produced in quantity for an all-in price of £125 including nickel lamps and purple plush seats. Most gratifying was the fact that the picture clearly showed an entirely different size of wheelbase.

After finishing my breakfast, I peered out of the window of our sitting room in Baker Street. The day was overcast and the sky above London steel grey. A snowburst seemed likely and I was glad to be indoors by a roaring fire. I had visited Bradleys tobacconist earlier when I had gone out to post a letter, and the easterly Siberian wind was still very much in evidence.

Holmes peered over the broadsheets of his newspaper as we heard the front door downstairs slam and Mrs Hudson's voice welcoming some poor frozen devil off the street. Not long afterwards the door to our sitting room burst open and Ralph Cosworth entered, fresh of face, holding his bowler hat and sturdy walking stick. He appeared in better spirits than our last encounter along Oxford Street, but refused coffee, saying he was en route to the Shoreditch works.

'Mr Holmes,' said he, full of excitement, 'yesterday evening I received an offer of £15 for my brougham from a young lady from Penge. Both my wife and I briefly discussed the proposal, but rejected it on account of us not yet having any knowledge of its full scrap value.'

'Ha-ha, a very judicious move, if I may say so,' chuckled my companion, relighting his long cherrywood pipe with a taper. Ralph turned his back to the fire and continued.

'Well, gentlemen, you can imagine our amazement – but a half hour later when Megan was putting our two children to bed, tucking them in if you will, the door bell clanged and a stocky man of about seven and thirty from Esher, claiming to be a grower of fir trees, Norwegian spruce, his modest business overwhelmed by demand at this time of year, requested to purchase our brougham for £25, whereupon he would break up the coach part, using only the wheelbase slightly modified to transport his Christmas trees to market. Once more, my wife and I seriously considered this proposal but declined, having decided to place an advert in the dailies and, by a process of elimination, accept the highest bidder.'

'Well, your business acumen is as sharp as ever,' said I.

'But that's not all, Doctor Watson, for the petite lady I told you about from Penge returned at half past eight, raising the total to a full hundred guineas. I confess we were flabbergasted by this generous offer and...'

'Refuse. You must refuse', said Holmes curtly, removing his pipe from his mouth and knocking it out on the hearth. 'You must on no account sell, Cosworth. I promise the sale and consequent removal of the brougham from your yard would be a grave mistake. Trust me, my dear fellow, a mistake that you would live to regret. The lady from Penge will conclude the deal when?'

'Why, Mr Holmes, she plans to visit my works this evening, at half past five. We will finalise payment in my office.'

'Rest assured, I and Doctor Watson shall also be in attendance. The lady from Penge intrigues me. I should be delighted to make her acquaintance. I strongly suspect she is not telling the entire truth concerning her interest in your brougham.'

* * *

That afternoon, round by the Bank of England in Threadneedle Street, I left Holmes promising to meet me later at St Paul's. He had an appointment with Jonathan Matthey & Co. and was to meet with the Managing Director in the board room for half an hour. Mycroft, Holmes's brother, had set the meeting up, but my companion also had a number of other firms he intended to visit. Procuring a cheap penny novel from the news vendor, I wandered round the City for a while, enjoying some refreshment in a nearby coffee house before heading for the Cathedral.

The wintry, overcast weather suited Sir Christopher Wren's monumental building and as I ascended the steep stone steps I looked forward to a short tour, taking in the Whispering Gallery and the Great Crypt where I wanted to visit Nelson's elaborate tomb.

Afterwards I sat in a pew over by the great door reading my book. Upon the fourth exciting chapter, I felt a tap on my shoulder and was delighted to see my old friend, wearing his cloth deerstalker and cape, leaning on his cane and looking very dapper and satisfied, for he had apparently gleaned much useful information concerning the case at hand. We went to Piccadilly for a roast beef lunch at Simpsons and thereafter took in a violin concerto at St James's Hall, the piano accompaniment first-rate.

We arrived at Cosworth's Metal Works in fine fettle and duly took our places discreetly behind a velvet curtain in Ralph's office.

Tilley Bagshaw, the lady from Penge, was a petite blonde, her hair gathered on top, her clothes of a presentable and fashionable type. She wore a winter bonnet and an overcoat over her skirts.

I was charmed the moment I saw her. She seemed intelligent and altogether a delightful creature. Cosworth greeted Mrs Bagshaw cordially and over tea the two discussed firstly the weather, the possibility of snow in the next few days, then moved on to more domestic topics. I listened from behind a section of curtaining to every word spoken. I knew this beautiful young lady was genuine, and that Holmes had been rashly mistaken in associating her with anything remotely underhand or unlawful. The more I listened to her prattling on about cacti, houseplants and her Scottie dog Findlay, the more I confess I liked her. Another cup of tea was poured and Cosworth too seemed enamoured, complimenting her on her winter bonnet and the pretty agate brooch she wore. Tilley Bagshaw informed him she had been visiting her sister Dora in Shoreditch and quite by chance noticed the black brougham on her way past the gates. She had fallen in love with the 'dear neglected old thing', as she referred to the monstrosity in the most flattering of terms. She enquired in the works office as to the present owner and was told Mr Cosworth was not at the factory but Mr Lamb, a workman, kindly proffered his home address.

Conversation eventually centred upon the more practical matter of payment for the brougham and how best to remove the carriage from the yard. Sherlock Holmes appeared suddenly from behind the curtain and introduced himself. I too came forward and blustered something about hoping very much the tea was to her liking.

A change in mood took place, and her sweet, gracious manner became flustered and annoyed. She got up to leave, the chair legs screeching across the linoleum.

'My dear Mrs Bagshaw, allow me to introduce myself. I am Sherlock Holmes, and this is my colleague Doctor Watson.' He moved forward to stop her leaving. 'A shame to break up our cosy little gathering just yet. Will you allow me to smoke? Now, to business.' His stern and uncompromising gaze appeared to unsettle her.

'My dear Cosworth, you will be aware Johnson & Matthey are a city firm of smelterers who deal in precious metals, platinum, silver, gold dust and bullion. Thanks to an acquaintance of mine on the board of directors I made enquiries and discovered the company audit office in Paul Street had records of a most eccentric order received from a Mr Pinnock of Pinnock & Porritt & Sons, solicitors acting for Cosgrove Senior of Cosgrove Metal Working. Gold ingots to the value of half a million pounds sterling were to be smelted down and processed, the moulds corresponding to four large carriage wheels and chassis. The gold should thus be drop-forged and encased in solid tubular steel. Halloa, the young lady appears in need of a handkerchief. Perhaps, Watson, you could lend her yours.'

'It is the truth,' she sobbed. 'I can verify all you have said, Mr Holmes,' said she, accepting my hanky, a sense of relief lightening her pixie features. I was genuinely concerned for her perilous situation for Holmes was like a tenacious hound who sensed blood.

'My name is Tilley Bagshaw. I live in Penge, not so far from Annerley Station. My husband Fred...' she paused, allowing for a fit of sobbing '...worked then for Johnson Matthey refining gold by the Miller chlorine method. The bullion work was carried out in another part of the foundry. One

163

day an operator reported sick and my husband was asked to take his place. Unusually, as you mentioned earlier, Mr Holmes, there were also specific moulds into which the refined gold would be poured. These corresponded exactly with four enormous carriage wheels and a chassis. As a direct consequence, both the front and rear axles of the black brougham are drop-forged from pure gold, the wheels and spokes also solid gold encased in tubular steel.'

'So the old brougham outside is worth a king's ransom. Why,' said Cosworth laughing, 'even King Midas would be proud to ride in it.'

'The coachbuilders Locketts also contributed their expertise,' added Holmes, smoking his cigarette furiously. 'It was they who supplied the second-hand carriage and specially constructed the hollowed-out wheels, shafts and so forth.'

But before any more could be said there was a loud commotion outside. We all rushed to the office window, foolishly allowing Tilley Bagshaw to make her escape, running down the stairs outside into the yard.

It was dark, but there was the glow of lamps from the factory. I saw a burly fellow wearing a long moleskin coat and low-brimmed hat, attaching horses and seizing the reins of the brougham. He jumped onto the driving seat and Tilley Bagshaw appeared, running as fast as she could across the yard. The fellow must have been strong and fit for he reached down with a muscular arm and hauled her up like a flailing rag doll. It was she who took the reins and, moments later, was lashing at the galloping horses.

The old black brougham clattered out of the factory gates and was gone, knocking over a coke brazier that spilled its fiery clinker across the pavement.

'A travesty,' remarked Holmes, gathering up his hat and coat. 'I thought better of her. Pure greed and the false certainty that they are bound to get away with it. The Bagshaws have placed themselves in very deep water. So the object all along was to steal the carriage. Watson, my dear fellow, where did they say?'

'Annerley.'

* * *

By taking a South Croydon-bound train from Victoria we managed to intercept them at Upper Norwood. We strode along the Crystal Palace Parade, lit by its rows of gas lamps, crowded at this time of night with omnibuses, lighted trams and the busy throng of pedestrians returning from work. Beyond the railings was the park and the mighty glass and iron structure housing the Great Exhibition.

'Ah, my dear Watson, see where the roads converge onto the Parade, their most likely route up the hill from East Dulwich, and I would expect them here presently. Halloa, there goes the brougham, Watson. See Mr and Mrs Bagshaw on the box seat? As I suspected, they are headed for Park Road, Annerley Hill being far too steep and slippery, the electric trams a hindrance.'

We hastily summoned a cab and set off in hot pursuit.

At Penge, at the beginning of Maple Road, we

tore along by the market at a cracking pace, rattling past the moveable stall-carts hauled out early each morning to their allotted pitches.

The umbrella man, the fruit and veg merchants, the flower lady, the knife grinder, the goose and turkey vendor, the Christmas tree seller, the china and glassware and pots and pans lady, were all apparently doing a roaring trade, for the place was crowded with folk in search of a Yuletide bargain.

Our tenacious cabman had indeed earned his extra shilling by the time we trotted at an altogether more leisurely pace up Maple Road toward the bottom end of Annerley Hill. It became evident that the Bagshaws were nearing home and did not suspect us of being in pursuit, their single goal being to reach Penge quickly; now they would go about concealing the carriage and thereafter dismantling it.

We turned into Jasmine Grove and there was a fresh development. From the glow of the carriage lamps we could see the vehicle had turned into some concealed driveway. We paid off the cabman and continued our pursuit on foot. The Grove was lined with sycamore and horse-chestnut trees. There were a number of fine large houses across the road. On our side a tall, slatted fence led to an entranceway.

'Hush,' exclaimed my companion. 'Not a word, Cosworth. Tread carefully, we have a gravel driveway to contend with where our boots shall make a fearful noise. Keep close, Watson, and make for the side of the building where that group of rhododendron bushes flourish so admirably.'

We were facing a red brick Methodist chapel, no

longer in use for prayer meetings, but converted recently to form some kind of warehouse. The brougham had been hidden inside as were the horses, so there must have been stabling also.

We managed to creep across to the clump of bushes. There was a pile of crates stacked against a drainpipe and Holmes clambered up to peer through the dingy chapel window.

Petite Mrs Bagshaw appeared at the side door like a fleeting ghost and walked briskly across to the large house next door, took a key from her purse, unlocked the front door and disappeared inside. I confess I much admired her gumption. She must have known much about the nature of galloping horses and riding carriages in general to have survived the frantic journey from the City to Penge without injury.

'My dear Watson,' my companion hissed from above. 'I do believe Frederick Bagshaw plans to unscrew the four large wheels. There is a brick-built blast furnace close at hand. No doubt he hopes by dawn to have smelted the gold into more manageable bars, easier to sell on the open market. I should say the fellow is most likely a man of the Veldt, of Dutch descent, a farmer's son, diversifying into the mining of precious metals, a long and fruitful apprenticeship. Just look at those great ham fists and muscular biceps. That's hard and industrious work for you. He would do ten rounds bare-knuckle fighting with the heavyweight champion Jem Fowler and win by a knockout. However, the healed scars upon his broad shoulders indicate a spell in Jo'burg Prison, for misdemeanours unknown, followed by a swift passage to England by steamer. Halloa, now is our time to intervene for he is wholly concerned in lighting the blast furnace and his back is facing us. The front doors, hurry.'

We all three of us stormed the old Methodist chapel, no doubt rented from the Union by Mr Bagshaw.

Holmes raced forward and delivered a sharp, stinging blow to the broad shoulders of the giant with his specially reinforced cane. I instinctively reached into my overcoat pocket for my service revolver but there was no need, for a violent struggle was to be avoided.

All his dreams of untold wealth in tatters, Bagshaw calmly turned round to face us and in good fellowship shook us each by the hand. The impressively built Adonis sporting a head of tousled blond hair and a ruddy, sunbaked complexion evidently had no intention of putting up a fight.

'Tilley told me about you, Sir. Are you detectives?'

'We are independently-minded enthusiasts of detection,' corrected my companion. 'I and Doctor Watson here are known to Scotland Yard certainly, but in a consulting capacity.'

'I guess filching the old fella's gold to make me rich was just a mirage,' said he, welcoming his wife who had returned from the house next door bearing a tray of victuals. Bread, cheese, onions and a jug of beer. Mrs Bagshaw smiled weakly at us.

'I promised Tilley we should travel the globe and have a country estate, a villa on the Riviera, wealth, privilege and anything her pretty heart desires.'

'And you very nearly succeeded,' admitted

Cosworth, handing out cigars. 'If not for Mr Holmes here, I should have been none the wiser, parting with the old brougham for a hundred pounds, glad of the money. As it is, I have my fortune restored in the most dramatic manner. The works can carry on producing wrought-iron railings and garden furniture, and our annual festive lunch at the Stag and Hounds can go ahead.'

'What a game of snakes and ladders it's been,' said Mr Bagshaw, enjoying smoking his cigar, thinking it well deserved.

'Anyhow, my father's to blame. If he had not lost his mind at the end, none of this would have happened,' admitted Cosworth.

'So when are the police to be informed and my wife and I arrested?' said Bagshaw.

'Ha, my dear fellow. Arrests? There shall be none on this occasion, I assure you,' said Holmes, leaning on his cane. 'You are from South Africa I take it, Mrs Bagshaw?'

'You are perfectly correct, Mr Holmes. It may not surprise you to learn that our real name is Van Outen. We are descended from Dutch settlers who farmed the Veldt. We met at my father's ranch in South Africa where my family breed horses, rear beef cattle and grow grapes. Alas, a misunderstanding during the movement of a consignment of bullion at a gold mine left my husband falsely accused of shooting a native African overseer. A spell in Jo'burg Prison followed from which he managed to escape. We were married and fled the country soon afterwards.'

10

The Arrest of Mortley Adams

The warm summer sunshine poured through the windows of our rooms in Baker Street, rainbow colours dancing upon the starched white linen of the tablecloth, beams of sunlight reflecting amongst the glassware, silver cruets, cutlery and toast rack laid so fastidiously by Mrs Hudson earlier.

My companion, Mr Sherlock Holmes, was lounging in his purple dressing gown. He had been up since dawn and was at present consulting a number of hefty calf-bound reference books.

'My dear Watson,' said he, hardly looking up. 'I have received a telegram. A notable collection of Russian jewelled eggs by Fabergé has been stolen from a house in Berkshire. Be kind enough to read it for me, will you.'

I imagined the house in question to be a great mansion set in a park owned by those with aristocratic connections to the Tsar and Tsarina residing in St Petersburg. In fact the telegram was from a Mr Theolodius Baines who lived at 'The Larches' in Maidenhead.

'Fabergé eggs. Where's the connection?' said I.

'My dear fellow, Mrs Baines is directly related to

the late opera diva Conietta De Carlo, who was her grandmother. The jewelled eggs formed part of a settlement in a will. Their provenance is impressive,' said he, folding over another page of his book. 'They were a gift to De Carlo from her mentor, the wealthy opera impresario Tonti, just prior to her triumph at La Scala Milan in Mozart's *Cosi Fan Tutte.*'

I had been fortunate to listen to a wax recording of De Carlo singing Schubert, capturing her majestic soprano voice for posterity.

'Incidentally, my dear Watson, the Fabergé jewelled eggs can be traced back to the Moscow coronation of Tsar Nicholas for whom they were originally commissioned.'

'Well,' said I, tossing the message aside. 'I should very much like to attack my own egg.'

'No time,' chuckled Holmes, knocking out his pipe.

'I'd rather finish my breakfast,' I insisted.

'My dear fellow,' answered Holmes, shrugging aside his dressing gown and revealing that he was already immaculately dressed and ready to travel. 'I have ordered a cab for half past nine. Marylebone Station is our destination and we must take the next available train to Berkshire, for if you had consulted the message properly, you would realise that Mr Theolodius Baines is to meet us at Taplow Station at noon.'

* * *

Our cab rattled down the Marylebone Road and drew up beneath the iron marquee sheltering the three-storey terracotta façade of the terminus, the Hotel Great Central facing opposite.

We hurried through the crowded concourse to the platform at the far side of Marylebone Station and were in plenty of time to board the next Beaconsfield and Princes Risborough train. We took a first-class smoker and, replete with a bundle of daily papers from the news vendor and a plentiful supply of tobacco, could want for nothing. The passenger service left Marylebone on the hour and in no time we were rattling through the suburbs towards Didcot. We passed through Oxfordshire and in about an hour and a quarter alighted at Taplow, a rural evergreen station on the borders of Buckinghamshire and Berkshire, not far from Old Windsor.

We were met by Theolodius Baines, a young man of presentable appearance. He wore a good quality worsted shooting jacket, plus-fours and brown creaky boots. He was a gentleman farmer who had lived in Maidenhead all his life. Like me, he had been wounded out of the Army but had been a commissioned officer in the Royal Engineers.

We were soon galloping in his horse and trap down a steeply wooded rise, which came out onto a main thoroughfare leading to the town and Maidenhead's ancient road bridge overlooking the Riverside Hotel and timber-fronted restaurant so popular with weekenders at this time of year.

A dusty turning led us past fields of wheat, flax and barley to an attractive timbered farmhouse with an outbuilding used as Mr Baines's office. Beyond were cattle sheds and a silo, and a number of agricultural machines.

We were met at the porch by Mrs Sophie Baines, who took our hats and coats and led us into the cool of the drawing room. A fine figure of a woman, she possessed a springy mass of frizzled hair, jet black and tied back in a bun. She had a healthy apple-blossom complexion born of good country air and no doubt helping out on the farm. She gave Holmes and myself a warm and affectionate smile and was desperately grateful to us for having come all the way from London at such short notice. On a small round table was waiting a tray of iced lemonade and we were further greeted by Hugo, a black Labrador gun dog, shivering and thumping his tail on the Turkey carpet.

'Well,' said I, patting the affectionate hound. 'I believe Old Windsor's but a few miles distant.' I took out my pipe and ship's tobacco and settled in a chair by the homely hearth.

'Oh indeed, Doctor Watson,' chortled Mrs Baines, passing me a napkin for my chilled glass. 'They make quite a tourist trap of the castle, so I hear. Droves of carriages clutter Windsor High Street on a Sunday.'

'By the by,' asked Holmes, 'have you received any callers recently? Retired conductors, musicologists, critics or anyone purporting to have known your grandmother in life, or perhaps a complete stranger?'

'Why, yesterday two most kindly religious gentlemen passing out tracts, a Mr Mortley Adams and a Silas Lovebringer, they stopped by and we chatted for some time about the temperance movement and the welfare of orphans in the East End. Mr Adams was a wonderfully eloquent speaker and I was quite the captive audience. We even prayed together for a short while. Theolodius was at the time visiting Beaconsfield on business concerning livestock.'

My companion drummed his long fingers on the arm of the chair. 'At any stage did either of these gentlemen, for whatever reason, choose to leave the room?'

'Mr Mortley Adams wished to freshen his face, for it was a beastly hot and dusty day and they were travelling on to Amersham. The bathroom is upstairs and of course I gave the gentleman directions while serving tea in the kitchen.'

'A mistake, a grave error of judgement,' said Holmes. The poor lady seemed at a loss for words.

'Presumably the safe from which the collection of Fabergé eggs was stolen was on that floor?'

'In my dear husband's study, Mr Holmes.' She began to sob and her husband was anxious to comfort her.

Holmes leaned forward to reassure her, his voice losing its sarcastic edge and becoming gentler and less caustic.

'My dear Mrs Baines, I can assure you that you are not the first person, nor indeed will you be the last, to be duped in such a deceitful way, the thieves taking full advantage of your unsuspecting and trusting nature. However, this said, let us shed no more tears and swiftly re-establish the facts beholden to this most singular case. A description of these two pious gentlemen, if you please.'

'Well, Mr Holmes, I can best describe Mr Mortley Adams as a tall individual, aged about six and twenty with elfin ears, a pronounced wobbly Adam's apple, and an entirely bald head. He wore the usual clerical garb. Ah yes, and was possessed of a lazy, permanently stuck left eye. I wondered if perhaps it were false and fashioned out of glass like a toy marble.'

'Quite exceptional observations, Mrs Baines. You have furbished us with a very reasonable description of the first fellow. What of Mr Silas Lovebringer?'

'Rather ape-like, short, squat stance, bristly eyebrows, somewhat mousey straight hair protruding from a floppy tweed cap. Black bushy beard.'

'A theatrical disguise if ever there was one, Watson. Thank you, Mrs Baines, now if I may...'

'Oh, and his suit did not quite fit properly. And his dog collar was askew, and he had a pair of muscular arched thighs,' she interrupted, pursing her lips together seriously.

'Bow-legged to the best of your knowledge. Was the fact that the late opera singer's collection of Russian eggs was kept in a safe at your house in Berkshire ever made known to the public?'

'Why, Mr Holmes, only last month *The Ladies' Voice*, a popular journal, ran an article about my late grandmother Conietta De Carlo's career as an opera singer. It mentioned the opera impresario Tonti, who was her lover as well as mentor. And the gift of the Fabergé eggs. It also gave details of my house and the fact I had inherited them.'

'*The Ladies' Voice* has a wide enough circulation to cause concern. Why, every jewellery thief in the metropolis should have been alerted.'

'Oh Mr Holmes, those eggs are of such sentimental

value. I should never have wanted them sealed away in some bank vault. They are a keepsake to be enjoyed.'

'Alas, others would view the late diva's precious set of Fabergé eggs with no sentiment whatsoever,' said Holmes brusquely. 'The monetary value alone of the blue stones, the clusters of diamonds and rubies, would be bound to attract certain criminal masterminds whose only objective is to steal the miniature decorative eggs, break them up and re-set the stones at great profit. There are several such gangs in the East End that I know of, willing to run the risks.'

'Oh my poor, dear grandmother would turn in her grave. Break them up, you say?'

'Certainly. Your grandmother's cherished heir-looms would thus be lost to the legitimate market forever, so we have little time and I must bring to bear some of the considerable knowledge I have acquired while working on similar cases. Watson, have you some strong tobacco handy? My own supply somewhat dwindled on our train journey from Marylebone.'

'Of course, my dear fellow.'

I passed over my ship's tobacco and observed Holmes swiftly recharge his cherrywood pipe before striking a match.

'Capital. Well, Mr Baines, you've informed the local constabulary, I trust?' asked my companion, occasionally puffing on his pipe in a leisurely way.

'Reluctantly that is the case, although I would not personally trust those officious blockheads to tie my bootlaces, let alone investigate the theft of my wife's Fabergé eggs,' said Theolodius Baines. His dog plodded over to rest his friendly paws at his master's feet.

'Our thieves will no doubt assume the local police have been alerted, and that plain-clothes officers are patrolling the town and keeping a watchful eye on the railway stations. The Berkshire force do not employ total incompetents, Mr Baines, and they may yet prove crucial to bringing this odious Mortley Adams and Silas Lovebringer to justice. But for now the game's afoot and myself and Doctor Watson here are about to join the fray. The farm buildings, cattle shed and so forth? I should like to examine the area.'

'Along the concrete path, turn right, Mr Holmes, you shall come across my old plough and a wagon under wraps.'

While we were visiting the stock shed, at this time of day empty of cows and the stalls clean and tidy, Mr Marner, the farm manager, happened to mention by way of conversation that a prize sow, Myrtle, had gone missing, possibly wandered off beyond the stockyard fence into the surrounding fields. By now they would normally have located her but he confessed the pig was nowhere to be seen and he feared for her safety.

'She might even be dead for all I know,' said he, sadly.

'A pity. A good breeder is invaluable,' said I, fully sympathising.

'Indeed, for she is a prize Barnchester spotted pig. Tiny tusks and a porcine belly of considerable dimensions.' He paused to smoke a cigarette but, upon seeing his employer Theolodius Baines approaching the shed with a number of gentlemen, hurriedly stubbed it out on the concrete floor and got on with his duties around the farm.

The gentlemen, it turned out, were a group of police officers, members of the Berkshire force, and my companion was quick to request information concerning the case.

'Pray, what have you gleaned so far?' he asked, impatiently tapping his cane upon the concrete floor.

'We have established that two strangers were seen in Maidenhead last week, asking directions to the farm and the whereabouts of "The Larches". The landlord of the White Hart gave us a fair description – one tall, the other short.'

'Humph,' said Holmes, 'nothing more succinct – colour of hair, eyes, facial blemishes, stoops or limps, clothes worn?'

'Oh no sir, he seemed vague upon the finer points.'

'Well, we have a little to go on with. At least you secured the railway stations, sergeant?' asked Holmes, pacing up and down.

'At Maidenhead, certainly sir. The other local stations of Marlow and Taplow are deemed rural halts of little significance. We have men posted at Maidenhead Bridge.'

'But the nearby station?'

'What station, sir?'

'Taplow. We ourselves alighted there. A stopping service to London runs every hour.'

'Well, yes sir, but Taplow falls under the Buckinghamshire force and is beyond our jurisdiction.

The boundary between the counties is firmly laid down.'

'No buts, man. Watson, I think we shall return to Taplow Station at once and enquire of the porter whether anyone of Mortley Adams's description has passed through its portals recently.'

My companion leaned upon his cane and gazed wistfully out into the stockyard.

'If you don't object, Mr Baines, we shall require your excellent horse and trap for a little excursion up the hill.'

'I shall fetch it at once,' said he.

* * *

So here we were once more, enjoying a breezy sunny day in Berkshire, rattling along in the horse and trap, the nags doing a fair canter and I looking forward to a good lunch at the Riverside Restaurant in Bray. I felt we had amassed little in the way of useful evidence so far, but Holmes's instincts I knew were keen and he had honed in on some possibilities concerning the case.

At Taplow we bid Theolodius Baines adieu and entered the ticket hall of that picturesque rural station. I strolled out onto the sunny platform full of the lazy drone of bees settling on the sweet-pea flower baskets and window boxes full of colourful blooms. I observed by the sign-board there was ten minutes before the next stopping service to London.

Holmes tugged at my sleeve, directing my gaze to a long, oblong box and we respectfully removed our hats, for outside the parcels' office was a coffin on a platform trolley, partly covered in a canvas sheet to protect the polished elm beneath. The freight of coffins on the railways was a common occurrence and caused no undue comment. However, my companion could not resist examining the official label with his magnifying lens and I saw the enlarged wording 'Lunnon, Marylebone – to be collected by the undertakers'.

'Well, some poor devil shall not require to purchase a ticket,' said I. We were about to walk past the waiting rooms to the end of the platform to enjoy the fine view when a porter made an appearance and began sweeping nearby.

'Watson,' said my companion, taking out a cigarette. 'Pray what is the most noticeable feature of that most conscientious employee of the railways?'

'He sweeps with an awkward stoop, grips the short broom handle like his life depended on it, for he is tall and lanky,' said I.

'No, no, I meant the facial features, my dear fellow. Pray, do you recall Mrs Baines's minute description of Mortley Adams?'

Careful not to alert the porter's suspicions and anxious he should not be privy to our conversation, I joined Holmes behind the departures board and studied the fellow from afar.

'The right eye feverishly darts this way and that while the left pupil remains motionless, staring ahead. There can be only one explanation – the eye is false and made of glass.'

'Bravo. Ah, what have we here?' I heard the muffled blast of a train whistle in the distance. The parcels' office door had creaked open and I was dumbfounded to see a bow-legged individual with Neanderthal features bearing a menacing steely gaze lope over to the trolley and check beneath the canvas sacking. He grunted and hurried back into the parcels' office, and then came back outside again as if undecided about something.

'Silas Lovebringer, we meet at last,' muttered Sherlock Holmes. 'See how our nosey chimp seems unduly concerned about the coffin, checking beneath the canvas again and again. Halloa, now Mortley Adams acting the role of the porter abandons his broom beside the fire bucket. Now they both return to the office and shut the door. Watson, this is a most singular deception for they aim to stow that coffin in the guard's van of the incoming train and see it safely on its way to Marylebone.'

The London-bound locomotive slid into the country station, dispensing billowing clouds of steam and smoke about the platform. A sweet little lady struggling with a hefty pair of suitcases was the only person to leave the train. However, no porter came forward to offer assistance and she was rightly perplexed. Brandishing her ticket in a state of some annoyance, she walked past the deserted porter's lodge and was soon lost to view.

Mortley Adams and his accomplice reappeared wearing civilian attire, looking for all the world like ordinary passengers about to board a train – which they were about to do.

The guard, noticing the coffin outside the parcels' office with its attendant label, got out of his van, went over to the trolley and began pushing it up the platform past the gentlemen's and ladies' waiting rooms.

'Here, give us a hand.' He spoke to Silas Lovebringer who was wearing a 'loud' checked suit and bowler, popular with the turf and boxing fraternity. Mortley Adams, looking equally bright and gaudy, rushed forward to help push the trolley and convey the coffin into the luggage van.

'Where's old Jacob, I wonder?' said the guard irritably. 'Sleeping off his lunchtime jug of beer. Look at that, nobody on duty to collect tickets either. I know it's a rural stop and he tends the flower baskets, tubs and window boxes with a watering can, but a proper porter should make more of an effort to carry out his duties in the middle of nowhere. Where on earth has the old fella got to?'

For myself, I imagined poor Jacob, far from inebriated, was bound and gagged in one of the wash-rooms, but before I could express my alarm, Holmes bundled me into a second-class carriage and the train was soon steaming off towards Marylebone, Taplow left far behind.

While we rattled along I considered the fact that both thieves were at present sat in the next compartment and that the coffin they were so interested in was safely stowed in the guard's van.

Charging his pipe with tobacco, perched in the corner of the carriage like a bird of prey, Sherlock Holmes beckoned me closer and spoke with some urgency.

'Watson,' said he, 'have you your service revolver handy? Mortley Adams and his wily accomplice Silas Lovebringer are part of some scheme involving a wider web of criminality. Surely there will be bogus undertakers and a hearse awaiting delivery of the coffin at the Great Central railway terminus at Marylebone Station. On no account must we let that coffin be carried beyond the porter's kiosk.'

'Do you want me to shoot pigeons?' said I.

'Your good humour is on this occasion a trifle unwarranted. We are, my dear Watson, about to enter a most dangerous arena of criminal activity and we are sure to come face to face with a violent gang of East End crooks. The precious Fabergé eggs are worth killing for, Watson, so we must be on our guard at all times once the train enters the London terminus.'

I lost no time checking my trusty service revolver and spent the remainder of the journey gazing out at the passing scene, the spires of Oxfordshire, the picturesque stretches of countryside, until we reached the suburbs of London and the train slowed down a little. My companion seemed to be deep in thought, smoking his pipe, oblivious to the thick clouds of tobacco smoke filling the compartment with a poisonous reek that even a partly opened window could not entirely dispel.

And it was at Marylebone Station that the most dramatic events were to unfold for I was privileged to play a significant part in the downfall of Mortley Adams and the eventual scattering of a ruthless gang of gem thieves based in Hackney, east London.

Amid the ever-present tang of stale locomotive smoke, the bustle of passengers and the shrieks and whistles of porters and baggage staff, from behind a cart heaped high with postal sacks, I and my companion Sherlock Holmes observed the coffin being unloaded and wheeled along the platform towards the ticket entry stand. There was a gentleman in black wearing a top hat in the far distance, presumably the bogus undertaker.

Following at some distance behind the coffin was Mortley Adams, strutting like a peacock, his bowler at a rakish angle, and beside him the apish, hairy fellow, always grunting.

'Mr Crotchett from Crotchett & Wimpole & Son has informed me the Hearse will be waiting outside,' said a self-important railway official with long side-whiskers and grizzled hair. 'Careful with the bier, Mr Trenchard.'

Holmes leapt out from behind the postal cart and delivered a striking blow to the coffin. The porter and pompous railway superintendent were stopped short and initial confusion turned to anger.

'What the devil's the meaning of this, sir?' he said.

'You will be so good as to alert Inspector Braun over at the office of Transport Police, this card will confirm my credentials. Tell him we will require a number of stout constables to assist in an arrest. Not only of the bogus undertaker Mr Crotchett, but also of these two gentlemen dressed in "loud", tasteless checked suits and bowlers. They should be securely handcuffed. You would do well in a circus as a clown, Mr Adams. And Silas here could act as your performing chimp. Now don't move, or Watson shall not hesitate to blow your brains out over the platform. He is a keen shot and rarely misses.'

I glanced round and caught sight of the fellow in the black frock coat and top hat. He appeared to look anxious and was arguing with a station official, who would not let him through.

But it was then that something began stirring inside the coffin. Each of us heard a loud scratching noise as though sharp fingernails were raking the underside of the lid.

'What abomination is this?' uttered a passing cleric, hastening away.

Sherlock Holmes lost no time. He slung aside the canvas and using all his considerable strength worked at the lid of the coffin with his specially strengthened cane.

'My dear fellow, no fancy brass plaque or fitments, this is a bare, functional box, I must say.'

I kept my revolver aimed at the two thieves and marvelled as Holmes with a flourish prised the lid off and flung it aside, whence it clattered onto the platform, useless and wrecked. But it was what was actually inside the coffin that caused the most outrage, for it was no wizened, yellow corpse that greeted us but a rather plump and inebriated-looking pig curled up on straw.

'It's Myrtle, the prize Barnchester pig that went missing from the farmyard!' said I.

'Fed a large amount of bran mash and bottled beer to sedate her. My dear fellow, the Barnchester pig's value has soared immeasurably. Myrtle is worth dead or alive half a million at least.'

'Good Lord, so she was fed the miniature Fabergé eggs with her usual bran mash,' said I. 'The old girl has eaten a dinner of blue stones, diamond clusters and rubies, the ornate bases of the eggs being disposed of.'

186

'Bravo, my dear Watson. You are correct on all accounts. Porkers have a most sturdy digestive system that can cope with all manner of delicacies. So Mortley Adams and his associates, including our undertaker friend who I see has been handcuffed and led away by Transport Police, originated this cunning scheme by which means a valuable collection of Fabergé eggs might be smuggled out of Berkshire and transported across London at no risk of being detected.'

'Mr Holmes!' Mortley Adams shouted as he and the others were led away. 'But for you I should be a rich man.'

Loping along like a chained animal, Silas Lovebringer snarled and grunted, beside himself with rage.

'And now you and your friend here are facing a long spell in prison, oakum picking,' quipped one of the constables as we approached the station concourse.

11

The Hampstead Heath Mystery

Glancing at a page of my journal, I recall a particularly ingenious and memorable crime perpetrated on the London Underground Railway.

It occurred during the evening rush hour. A train left Hampstead Station and was entering the tunnel when a message was relayed to the station master, a Mr Barham, by means of a frantic bell telegraph, that a person was lying prone on the rails in the tunnel between Hampstead and Golders Green stations. The next southbound train at Golders Green was halted and did not proceed. The northbound train then accelerating at a speed of 15 mph, came to a halt midway through the tunnel at a stop signal. During this interlude, while the underground train was stationary, a pair of ginger-haired, dandified fellows wearing 'loud' and extra-ordinary checked trousers, grey frock coats and top hats, who according to one passenger shockingly wore face powder and the faintest application of make-up, leapt into the central gangway of the middle car and confronted a dignified gentleman sat opposite, by firstly pointing a loaded revolver at his head and, next, snapping with a pair of powerful pliers the handcuff chain around his wrist that secured a leather Gladstone bag.

No commotion ensued. Commuters remained passive, reading their evening newspapers. It was all over very quickly. The ginger dandies apologised profusely to the passengers for any inconvenience caused. The doors to the middle car opened as if by magic – in fact the guard of the train was also being harassed by a ginger dandy with a gun and obligingly forced to operate the mechanical hydraulics – and all three of the gang leapt down onto the track and were soon lost to the musty, claustrophobic darkness of the tunnel.

The Gladstone bag belonged to a Mr Joshua Cohen, a regular commuter on the line. It happened to contain over £100,000 worth of De Beers rough-cut diamonds, Mr Cohen being a dealer in precious stones with offices at Hatton Garden.

Both tunnel entrances, one at Hampstead and the other at Golders Green, were sealed off. No one, apart from railway staff and a number of constables of police, were seen either leaving or entering the tunnel. Inspector Lestrade, who was in charge of the investigation, believed the gang had adopted a new disguise as railway workmen and made their escape during the confusion using the northbound platform of Hampstead Station. The body slumped over the rails that had caused the initial alert turned out to be a dummy filled with straw wearing – and this was particularly galling to the inspector – a ginger wig.

Barely had the popular press, much to the evident chagrin of Scotland Yard, trumpeted front-page headlines, such as 'Perfect Crime Committed on the Underground Railway', when along came whole pages devoted to matrix diagrams, informative 'cut-away' plans and isometric reconstructions of the tunnel showing the infamous section between Hampstead and Golders Green, something not altogether lost to readers, including myself and Mr Sherlock Holmes, being the fact that roughly 300 yards north of the station the Hampstead line runs no less than 250 feet below the crest of Hampstead Heath.

Who was the criminal mastermind behind such an audacious enterprise, and how on earth had such an operation been planned?

It was a very glum and serious Inspector Lestrade who visited our lodgings in Baker Street. Upon realising he was about to undergo the most embarrassing and much publicised defeat of his career, he had called on his old acquaintance in the hope that some leeway in the case might be obtained.

'Well, Mr Holmes, I am absolutely at a loss. All I have is an old ginger wig and a scarf recovered from the trackside and a bout of bronchitis from having walked every inch of those damned tunnels.'

'Pray, let us firstly examine this fluffy old affair of horsehair under my magnifying lens. Watson, a whisky and seltzer all round. Cigars are in the coal scuttle, Inspector.'

My companion adjusted the gas jet on the globe lamp and drew his chair closer to the table.

'Upon closer inspection, I observe a label for Fossey's the theatrical wigmaker in Shaftesbury

Avenue. I find a long strand of fine, blonde hair snagged to the ginger wig's lining. The scarf is of particular interest. Pray, what does it smell, of my dear Watson?'

'Perfume,' said I.

'To be more precise, "Eau de Violette" by Floris. Its faint fruity undertones exquisite and most distinctive. In short, it is a premier range. It is expensive, one of the most expensive of the maker, favoured by privileged ladies and royalty. And what else have you for me, Inspector?' asked Holmes, lighting a cigarette.

'We found one of the stolen diamonds. It was at the side of the track. A constable luckily shone his bull's-eye lamp in that area of the tunnel. So far as my investigation is concerned it represents nothing of consequence. Obviously it was dropped by the gang as they headed along the tunnel towards Hampstead Station, disguised as railway workers.'

My companion carefully placed the tiny gemstone beneath the light of the gas lamp and meticulously studied every facet. I wondered the worth of such a stone. Mr Cohen I was certain would be grateful of its return.

'My dear fellow, you must not be too downhearted, for the diamond and the Floris perfume together now present us with certain unique possibilities.'

'Oh, and what are they?' he said morosely.

'We are dealing with a group of refined and resourceful young ladies, not a gang of ginger dandies. A propitious fate must have brought the three together.'

'Women!' Lestrade grew very red in the face. 'A

little joke at my expense, Mr Holmes? Shame on you. Is it not bad enough to be wholly flummoxed by a robbery?'

'To continue. The diamond detached itself from the crown of a ladies' earring while she was inside the tunnel. It is not a rough-cut diamond of the type carried by Mr Cohen in his Gladstone bag.'

'However,' said I seriously, 'where does that lead us, Holmes?'

'I have been making a study of certain of the maps and diagrams contained in this morning's edition of *The Telegraph*, all relating to the infamous underground robbery. I propose, my dear Watson, that upon finishing our whiskies and seltzers we, along with Inspector Lestrade here, summon a four-wheeler and head at once for Hampstead Village and the Heath. Wrap up well, for it will be fiercely chilly up there.'

* * *

Our four-wheeler trotted past Hampstead Underground, a group of village shops and a tea room. Many pedestrians were braving the cold wintry weather, flocking hither and thither along the high street. We proceeded along Heath End Hill; the road to the hilltop is steep and lengthy and at the brow we paid off the cabman and walked briskly down a lane possessing a row of pleasant homely houses, to the woods of hawthorn and ancient oak and sycamore, and a bridged pond.

The ornithologist knows Hampstead Heath's value and in a world increasingly bustling and progressive there is a curious fascination in so remote and deliberate a region situated north of the city, in which even in the finest weather a suggestion of desolation broods. As Holmes predicted, a strong and persistent wind blowing across the heathland made our trudge hard going. Inspector Lestrade was all for abandoning our walk and seeking out the nearest tea room, but my companion, I knew, had not led us up here simply for the exercise. Holmes at one stage raced down a grassy bank waving his cane enthusiastically in the air.

'Halloa, what's this?' I heard him say. Striding amongst the furze, knocking back a tangle of bracken, he directed our gaze to a ferro-concrete structure some distance away, partly concealed by dense undergrowth. With its dome-shaped roof it reminded me of a hide used by parties of birdwatchers.

'Are we to spend the entire afternoon trying to spot a crested grebe?' Lestrade quipped, taking out his cigarettes.

'On the contrary, this is how they got down to platform level and gained access to the tunnel system,' said Holmes, walking about, tapping the concrete base of the structure with his cane. 'See here, a new, shiny Yale lock attached to the bolt of a small wooden door. No sign of rust or wear.'

'What on earth is it?' said I.

'A ventilator, Watson. There is the platform of the unused and abandoned Bull and Bush Station some distance below ground.'

I edged forward through the thick, tussocky grass until I reached the perimeter of the large concrete dome.

'I am still not clear on this,' said Lestrade, passing me a Woodbine from his packet.

'When the section of Northern Line beneath us was built, plans were laid for five stations: Chalk Farm, Belsize Park, Hampstead, Bull and Bush, and Golders Green. What we have here, my dear Lestrade, is one of the original twelve-foot diameter working shafts retained to serve as a ventilator duct for the station beneath. Part-way through the building of Bull and Bush Station the Charing Cross, Euston Road and Hampstead Railway Company decided to shelve the project as the station was surplus to requirements. But the platforms remain.'

'Granted, but they must be an awful long way down, Mr Holmes.'

'By a combination of skilled mountaineering and use of galvanised iron ladders leading to the central fairing, and deep-sunk staircase wells already in place, the ventilator offers a perfect means of access and escape.'

'Women, you say? Surely this is beyond the bounds of their physical type? My dear wife would not even consider climbing a step ladder.'

'I should say at least one of the ladies is a professional mountaineer, well versed in the climbing of steep cliff faces. A certain amount of nerve and training is all that is required. Now, Inspector Lestrade, we will search out that delightful tea house I saw earlier upon the Heath and enjoy a spell of warmth and relaxation before once more entering the great metropolis in search of Shaftesbury Avenue and answers concerning a certain ginger-haired creation manufactured by Fossey & Co., theatrical wigmakers to the stars.'

* * *

An elderly, stooped man wearing a drab pair of breeches and buckled shoes, and a preposterous mousey wig to make him appear younger, proved most forthcoming.

'Indeed, sir, we manufactured ten ginger wigs for the production of Kenneth Paston's *Lives and Letters* running at the Wimborne Theatre, Drury Lane. They are created specially for its female lead, Miss Nancy Starr, who plays opposite Charles Lemon. The production has proved popular with audiences so far, and I have here in my order book a request for another ten. Such wear and tear on a nightly basis wears the fibres out. Nancy Starr, who plays the forthright Miss "M" must always look her best. Have any of you gentlemen perchance seen the production?'

'I think we will visit the box office and purchase tickets for tonight's performance,' said Holmes, bursting with enthusiasm. 'Nancy Starr, you say?'

'An actress at the top of her professional career, Ellen Terry adored her, as did Sir Henry Irving, who I believe was anxious to sign her up for one of his productions at the Lyceum. She started out in the chorus of *The Pirates of Penzance*, you know. Arthur Sullivan gave her her first big break as Koko in *The Mikado*, and she never looked back. Her grasp of the whodunit mystery play is in my mind unsurpassed. The hysterical way she stabs Lord Wisley in the bath before the curtain call in *Lives and Letters* never fails to bring the house down.'

Granted, Inspector Lestrade was not wholly understanding of my friend's methods but he was not slow to appreciate fine dining at Simpsons of Piccadilly, nor the purchase of balcony seats at the Wimborne Theatre for a performance of *Lives and Letters*, for he was a great admirer of Charles Lemon, the principal actor whose name and stage photographs, along with Nancy Starr, emblazoned the foyer and front of the building. Upon arrival at the Wimborne the most noticeable comment amongst theatre goers was how attractive was the actress and how her fiery red hair suited the part of the forthright Miss 'M' to a tee.

The first act passed well enough, although the plot appeared tediously familiar. A vicar, an elderly dame, an old doddering butler, Symes, a surly maid, an old duffer of a colonel, but Charles Lemon as Lord Wisley brought life to the play, and by the third and final act I was riveted to my seat, enjoying the shenanigans of the bounder Lord Wisley and his doting admirer, the forthright Miss 'M', whose sister's husband is mysteriously killed in a riding accident.

For the reader's interest, I have reproduced the final part of the script.

<u>Charles Lemon and Nancy Starr</u>
<u>Bathroom Scene, Final Act</u>

'Get out of here, Miss "M". I tell you I won't have you coming in here like this. I've told you already Pamela's husband was killed when his horse fell under him. I had nothing to do with it. Now get out of here before I call Symes.'

'How could you, Lord Wisley? I trusted you, I loved you, I would have done anything for you. You and Pamela going away together, I won't have it, I won't have it.'

'Put that knife away, Miss "M", d'you hear me? Put it down I say, you silly little minx.'

'I won't have it, Lord Wisley. You and Pamela.' *Loud screams.* 'Take that, and that ... and that, you cad.' *Lights dim, sobs of regret are heard.* 'I love you, Lord Wisley. I love you.' *Curtain falls.*

The night ended with raucous applause and many standing ovations. It was with mixed emotions that I queued along with other 'stage door Johnnies' at the side of the theatre, holding a bunch of carnations, waiting for Nancy Starr to make an appearance before being whisked off to the Ivy for a celebratory dinner. Holmes and Inspector Lestrade were also in close attendance. We had not long to wait. She flounced out in the latest fashions of the day and I caught a distinct whiff of Floris 'Eau de Violet' that went quite to my head. A smile for everyone and then she approached me, accepted her gift of flowers, and asked me if I had enjoyed the play. I was about to answer, when Holmes rushed forward, removed his silk top hat and asked in a smitten, grovelling voice, 'Eh Nancy, I mean Miss Starr, would you sign an autograph upon this piece of cigarette card? I have seen *Lives and Letters* thirty times and never tire of your perform-ance, or Kenneth Paston's lively production. Casting you as the forthright Miss "M" was a stroke of genius.'

'Why, thank you,' said she, accepting a proffered propelling pencil from Inspector Lestrade and scribbling:

'For my dear devoted admirer, upon his thirtieth visit to my play *Lives and Letters* at the Wimborne. With all best wishes in the world, Nancy Starr.'

'Oh, by the bye,' Holmes added in an off-hand way. 'I hear Miss Lucy Houghton is in town. According to *The Telegraph* the lady spent a year in Askan Province in the Himalayas with her devoted Sherpa attempting the summit of Sheenong. Miss Houghton is staying at Claridge's. She is a Buddhist, vegetarian and a firm advocate of feminist principles, is she not?'

Before the actress was bustled to her waiting cab in Drury Lane she gave Holmes a shocked and vulnerable look. I somehow sensed she realised that my companion had found her out.

The following morning Holmes was able to ascertain the address of Nancy Starr. He had disguised himself as a stage hand, and upon moving scenery, chatted to a doorman employed at the Wimborne and found out that the popular actress lived in Hampstead. When Inspector Lestrade visited he informed us that Joshua Cohen, the diamond dealer, lived next door.

After finishing our breakfast, Holmes and myself sat either side of the hearth before a roaring fire, perusing the latest edition of *The Times*. The continued flawed efforts of Scotland Yard to trace those responsible for the underground train robbery were still making headlines.

Inspector Lestrade, still not entirely sure where our investigation was leading and exasperated by Holmes's methods, was personally doubtful whether three ladies were responsible, for he felt it was too sophisticated and physically demanding a task for them to be involved in a crime of this nature. He thus returned to Scotland Yard, determined to follow another tack.

Casting my gaze briefly over the sports pages I was alerted by a timid knock at the door. Unannounced, an Oriental of barely five feet in height, brown as a nut and of a slender build, wearing a *dhoti* and baggy orange pantaloons, entered our rooms. She bowed at my companion without even having been introduced.

'Ah, Sherpa Sungi, you received my wire. Is Miss Houghton not available? I rather expected, given the severity of the matter, she would lose no time appearing here in person.'

'Oh, Mr Holmes, she most anxious to meet. Tea at Claridge's at half past three, at the restaurant. She be there along with Miss Starr and myself. I come to give you this.'

The tiny Sherpa passed me a beautifully tooled green Morocco casket. The gold-leaf inscription read: Cohen Associates, London & Johannesburg.

'And what should I do with it?'

'The rough-cut diamonds are to be given to you for safe keeping, Mr Holmes – it was all our wishes that you should take custody of them. They are all present.'

She bowed deeply and prepared to leave. 'Remember, Mr Holmes, half past three at Claridge's.

We will be there, I promise. But no police, that is Miss Houghton's only condition.'

'Very well, you have my word,' agreed Holmes, 'half past three it is.'

Putting down his pipe, he slung the casket of rough-cut diamonds into the coal scuttle, totally disinterested, not even bothering to check its precious contents.

'Well,' said I sombrely, for I knew what my friend was considering. 'In all honesty, Holmes, I have never in my life felt less inclined to assist in an arrest. Call me an old fool if you will, but the ladies have my complete admiration. The skill, the nerve, the supreme combined intelligence. The planning alone is worthy of going down in history as the greatest train robbery of all time. The very notion of turning them in seems loathsome.'

'I am in full agreement Watson. The value of these rough-cuts of Cohen's means little to me but I should like to ascertain the reason for the gem robbery in the first place. This meeting at Claridge's is our best means of finding out. Inspector Lestrade will remain completely in the dark from now on. We shall treat the case as confidential and answer only to our own consciences.'

* * *

Tea at Claridge's beneath sparkling crystal chandeliers, surrounded by gilt mirrors and in the presence of three vivacious and entertaining young ladies, I would not miss for the world. The conversation was polite and cordial, the Dundee cake and delicately cut cucumber sandwiches, the

201

scones, jam and potted cream, the fruit tartlets and other mouth-watering delicacies, consumed with relish.

'You see, Doctor Watson, I so wanted Kenneth Paston to adapt Wilkie Collins's *The Moonstone* for the stage. I even offered to put up the money to produce it, but it is a very long novel. I still live in hope. I have been an ardent devotee of mysteries for many years and adore Oscar Wilde and Henry James.'

'And I presume, Miss Starr, it was you who first came up with the preposterous idea of holding up a train on the London Underground?' asked Holmes, pushing aside his plate and lighting his pipe.

'Indeed Mr Holmes, I was lying awake one night fretting over how I should interpret the forthright Miss "M" in *Lives and Letters* and conceived the entire plot scenario in fifteen minutes. Miss Houghton, Lucy that is, is a dear friend who also lives in Hampstead, and together we decided upon whether such a robbery was possible, given the technical difficulties. Sherpa Sungi introduced me to certain Buddhist techniques to calm the mind and remain serene in adverse circumstances. Lucy of course was responsible for punishing fitness regimes and intense training in the Cumbrian mountains. The use of ropes for climbing and descending from a great height, the use of breathing exercises, the toning of the muscles – I owe it all to her.'

'But the brains behind the scheme were yours, darling,' smiled Miss Houghton, patting her hand.

'So you both live in Hampstead,' said I, accepting one of Miss Houghton's cheroots.

'Not far from the Heath. It was while out walking my dogs I first came upon the curious ventilation shaft that was to play such an important role in the Underground robbery. You see, Doctor Watson, I knew that old fellow Cohen next door was a diamond dealer with an office in Hatton Garden. This is what started me off for it was me who, one morning, over the fence, proposed I should so much like to own the biggest diamond in the world and have a ring made out of it. He was an old fool, a bachelor easily charmed and I suspected he believed I was romantically inclined towards him, something I did nothing to discourage. Anyhow, the bait was set, for one day he told me he should be personally honoured if he could bring to my house a selection of large uncut stones from which a piece of fine jewellery, like a ring, might be made, at my own expense of course! I knew him to be a creature of habit, commuting every evening from his offices in Hatton Garden to another branch office in Golders Green, from where he would return to Hampstead at around seven sharp. Sherpa Sungi took it upon herself to shadow the old man from work every evening for two weeks, making a careful note of his movements, including his favoured seat in the middle car of the Underground train.'

'Thus you simply arranged a time to view the gems,' said Holmes, 'and Mr Cohen complied.'

'Exactly.'

'But what I fail to understand,' said I, 'is the reason why you stole the rough-cut diamonds in the first place? Surely you all love and are successful at what you do. Is riches really an issue?'

'The issue here, gentlemen, is that Lucy, Sherpa Sungi, and myself are sympathetic to the Suffragette cause. I should not take it so far as Emily Pankhurst or want to go to prison for my long-held beliefs in women's liberation, but our aim, if one can call it that, was to use the rough-cut diamonds to help finance the Movement. I believe what we did was honourable and my only regret is that we were never allowed to benefit the cause of Suffragettes in this country.'

N.B.
The green Morocco bound casket containing the diamonds was sent second class by normal post office channels to Mr Cohen's Hatton Garden address – anonymously. The persons responsible for the robbery on the London Underground were never traced, and the case remains locked away in police files.

12

The Tong Lai Trading Company

In the year 1903 Mr Sherlock Holmes and I spent a fortnight in Cornwall, a couple of weeks in August at that sparkling Cornish seaport town of St Ives, at that time becoming increasingly popular with pleasure-seekers, for the railways allowed those of us from London and elsewhere to seek out this delightful holiday location.

We rented a holiday villa overlooking the harbour, with its dozens of little fishing boats and the golden bay. The first morning of our stay I had intended to explore the tiny art shops around the town's narrow alleyways, my erstwhile companion content to sit out on the sunny balcony reading and smoking, and writing up his case notes.

However, before I had even left the comfort of my armchair our lady help Mrs Edenbridge, a polite and amiable soul of good Cornish stock, informed us a gentleman caller was waiting, a detective of police, who had learned of our sojourn in St Ives and urgently required an interview with my colleague.

'Inspector Clark of the Cornish constabulary,' said he, a discernible tremor in his voice. 'I hate to drag you away from your holiday like this, Mr

Holmes, but we have discovered three bodies on a beach at Culbones Cove, not so far from Withypool Point. I'm unsure as to the exact cause of death and I would value a second opinion. I am at a loss, sir. No boats have gone down recently and there've been no reported shipwrecks.'

'Drowning remains a possibility,' said Holmes, filling his pipe.

'Indeed, but I must warn you, the injuries are substantial.'

'Well Holmes,' said I, smoking my own pipe, knowing full well I had some authority upon the subject. 'Asphyxiation in a death by drowning case is surely not that difficult to determine. I believe we shall be done by lunchtime.'

* * *

Leaving the pleasant prospect of St Ives, we headed around the peninsula in an open carriage, the horses making a brisk canter. The rugged coastline, with its hidden coves and secluded inlets, lay on one side, and shoreward, remote villages with tiny winding lanes gave way to a landscape of furze and heath, the road sweeping round to Withypool Point, a beach dominated by a narrow outcrop of rock. Culbones Cove was a little further on.

By way of steep steps cut into the cliff we were able to clamber on to the beach. I saw three bodies in the distance, which had the appearance of beached whales. Seagulls wheeled overhead as we trudged across the sand. My companion, wearing his deerstalker and travelling cape, prodded amongst the rock pools and together we negotiated a partly submerged granite groyne, slippery with green algae and fronds of seaweed.

'Halloa,' cried a sergeant of police, gingerly hopping from one rock pool to another to join us. He greeted Clark with an enthusiastic burst of Cornish amiability, but of us he was less enamoured.

'Hey-ho Clarkie, another fine day, plenty of 'un fishing smacks out there on the water. My brother's after a netful of pilchards and a bit o' lobster, so he tells me.'

'Good morning, Sergeant Bowlin. I should explain, these fellows are not from the coroner's office. May I introduce Mr Sherlock Holmes and this is his colleague Doctor Watson, both down from London.'

'Foreigners eh? Well, you'd best come 'n have a look 'un bodies. Old Abraham found 'em washed up on the rocks. Keeps going on about a tollin' bell. He lives 'un fisherman's cottage on the headland. Lor', Mr Clark sir, we'll 'ave charabanc loads 'un holiday visitors comin' t'gape 'n gawk from St Ives.'

'A tolling bell, you say?' asked Holmes.

'A ghost toll by all accounts, sir. It comes from the old church over at Zennor. A single toll announces the death of a sailor. A continuous tolling indicates a disaster at sea.'

'Yet another myth to add to that excellent collection of romantic Cornish legends. A folk tale I am sure, told in many a harbour tavern throughout the land, Sergeant Bowlin,' chuckled my companion.

'Abe Rowse said he heard 'un bell ringing 'un I believe him. He heard the bell tollin' the night before he found 'un three dead bodies.'

Officers were desperately trying to raise a canvas

sheet, but the stiff inshore breeze was hampering their efforts. Spumes of frothy spray rose into the air, crashing with a tremendous din along the shore. We approached the first body slumped face down in salty water, or at least what remained of it. Of particular interest to a doctor were the missing limbs and the torn skull, many fractures and lesions, a small tattoo, much faded, on the forearm.

'Orientals,' muttered Holmes, indicating Clark should come closer.

'Well, they was drowned 'un met their ends in the deep. I'd recognise a drowned man anywhere for one of my brothers, the eldest, perished off Newlyn when his boat went down, all hands lost. Customs men found the body on the rocks. That be twenty years ago now.'

'I beg to differ,' said Holmes, kneeling down, examining the human remains with his magnifying lens. Without due reverence or sentimentality he wrenched up the arm, turning the palm of the hand face up. 'Clark, you will observe the multiple powder burns. Minute splinters of wood embedded in the skin, as are fragments of stone chips.'

'Fish got at 'em. Lor', how the lobsters hereabouts love a corpse,' commented the police sergeant, unimpressed and wholly sceptical regarding my companion's methods.

'I should say this fellow is a Chinese, of an age of six and twenty. The muscle tone is quite superb. He would have been in life ultra fit and agile as a gnat. The tattoo evades me. A sign of luck perhaps.'

'But the cause of death?' implored the still mystified detective.

'The injuries are wholly consistent with an explosion of some kind, the Oriental's body later disposed of at sea and washed up by the incoming tide.'

'Remarkable,' said I. 'Thus we can safely assume the others met a similar fate.'

'Just so, Watson. Where was that place Abe Rowse mentioned in relation to the tolling bell?'

'Zennor,' answered Sergeant Bowlin. 'A tiny village further along 'un headland.'

'Then I believe, Inspector Clark, we shall leave Sergeant Bowlin in charge of matters pertaining to the removal of bodies, and continue our pleasant carriage trip round the peninsula. Watson, have you a cigarette handy?'

In fact, Clark later explained that the old church of St Modwen, to which Sergeant Bowlin referred, was not Zennor parish church, but an isolated Norman structure located high on the shaggy moor hills, given over mostly to colonies of seabirds.

Approached by a footpath, the tiny church with its squat bell tower I should describe as far too small to accommodate a full-sized congregation. There was but a scattering of leaning headstones amongst the tall grass of the unkempt churchyard. However, the view of the sea from that vantage-point was truly beautiful to behold.

Whilst I wandered about, pausing to study headstones mottled with yellow and white lichens, noting the emblems of mortality, the bleached, much-eroded skulls and scythes, and the angels and sail ships of fishermen's graves, my companion and Mr Clark took it upon themselves to try to enter the old church. This proved impossible. The sturdy door, made of oak timbers, weathered grey from centuries of buffeting coastal winds and salty air, was locked and barred.

We stood in the sunshine wondering what to do next when a sprightly, silver-haired old fellow sporting a tweedy suit and straw boater came up the path, walking his spaniel dog.

'I'm afraid the church is closed up,' said he. 'For as long as I can remember the church was open to all and sundry. It's in a state of disrepair, I grant you, with water dripping everywhere, and the old pews are mildewed, but it's a nice cool place on a hot day like this to rest your feet and recuperate after a long walk.'

'Is it Norman, fifteenth century?' asked Holmes, leaning on his cane, his tall frame casting a shadow over a nearby headstone.

'You are enthusiasts of church architecture, I take it. We had a party last week who were busy brass rubbing, a holiday club who had already visited the parish church at Zennor, popular with tourists. I think the structure is earlier, perhaps fourteenth century, being too small and impractical for clergy and congregation, situated so high up and difficult to get to. My name's James Sims by the way. I live just over there. You can see the pinkish tiled roof, and Mr Tong lives further along the path in the big house.'

'Ah, I see an opportunity,' chuckled my companion, heading round the side of the church.

'I'd fancy the vestry, as you will observe, has a buttress window without stained glass. If you gentlemen would care to take a supporting role and push me up?'

This we did, Mr Clark, myself and Mr Sims heaving him up towards the roof guttering. Once he had a foothold he clambered in through the vacant space. A short while later the oak door on the side of the church creaked ajar, and bidding Mr Sims farewell, for he was expected for lunch by his wife and had toured the old building often, we duly entered the vestry sanctum and were much surprised.

'Boxes and boxes and still more boxes,' murmured Clark, bemused at the warehouse look of the place. Boxes were stacked everywhere, and leaving the vestry we found that the aisle, nave, the ancient pews and the chancel were also utilised for storage. The boxes were uniformly one size, rectangular and constructed of stiff cardboard. There was not one single label in evidence.

Holmes was presently leaning over the stone font at the end of the church. We strolled along the aisle to join him.

'My dear Watson, the intricate carvings upon the font are quite clearly Norman, fourteenth century. And yet our font cover is constructed of iron, riveted round and plainly a heavy and cumbersome object, supplied with robust chain and pulley mechanism. It's hardly tarnished and apparently newly-cast. Mr Clark, would you be good enough to step over and tug the hemp rope over by the pulpit? Watson, he may require your assistance.'

Indeed, the rope was difficult to pull and eventually required the three of us to apply sufficient strain to create a loud ringing sound resonating in the belfry above.

'So, a bell also recently installed. Firstly we have the makings of a docklands warehouse, secondly the tolling a means of warning or perhaps more likely alerting others in the vicinity as a prearranged signal. The cost alone of casting a new font cover and bell would be prohibitive, thus we must assume the hundreds of boxes stored in this out of way place contain something of value.'

Mr Clark meanwhile, acting upon an impulse, carefully removed one of the boxes from the back of the nearest pile. The lids were not fastened and when he saw what lay inside he burst out laughing. 'Chinese firework rockets!' the inspector exclaimed.

'Welcome.'

We heard a quietly amused voice echo about the nave, and turned round to find the porch door wide open, bright summer sunshine flooding the aisle. A chubby Oriental gentleman stepped out of a golden shaft of sunlight and regarded us with some curiosity.

In the strong rays from the sun blazing through the open door, creating a glowing nimbus, he seemed to me to resemble an incarnation of the lord Buddha, for he possessed tremendous ears, an entirely bald head and a face of supreme tranquillity.

'I see you have stumbled on my little business venture. My name is Tong. I trade as Tong Lai Trading Company, all perfectly legal. I recently purchased this old church from the parish and put it to good use. St Modwen's flourishes again. My wife Lai knows more about the old building than

212

I, for it was she who first had the idea of using the modest profits accrued from my business to restore the whole for future generations of holiday visitors to enjoy. Please come outside and smoke a cigar. We saw you earlier and have prepared some ices and cold meats for your lunch. Mr Sims told me you were keen on church architecture.'

'Indeed,' said I. 'This Cornish church above the village of Zennor is well worth restoring. And the font cover is a start.'

'From small beginnings,' Mr Tong said, guiding us swiftly into the churchyard and locking the door behind him. From his cigar case he generously proffered one each for our enjoyment. They were Cuban and smoked deliciously.

'We imagined the place was derelict,' said Holmes good-naturedly. 'I myself climbed in through the vestry window. If we had realised it was private property I should never have dreamed of taking such liberties.'

'Perfectly understandable. Now follow me along the coast footpath, gentlemen. Watch your step. My house is down the slope and there are many rabbit holes to traverse. Lunch awaits and I am sure in this hot weather some refreshments are in order.'

Mr Sims was already sat outside on the veranda with his wife, enjoying a meal. As we trudged past we waved. I admit the heat of the day and our physical excursions in the church had worn me out, although I had a ravenous appetite and looked forward to meeting Mr Tong's wife Lai.

What a homely domestic scene awaited us – cushioned chairs, a table of victuals spread out before us, Oriental pickles, and cold chicken and salad. And seltzer water to quench our thirst. Mr Tong's wife appeared much younger than he, but her silver hair indicated they were in fact roughly the same age. Lai moved about with a grace and agility that belied her years and was most attractive to behold.

'Do you like our little church, Doctor Watson?' said she, passing me a serviette.

'I think the view of the sea from there is enchanting,' said I. 'You are very fortunate to live in such beautiful surroundings.'

'Mr Tong and I arrived here two years ago. I fell in love with this house and my husband's commitments as an industrialist in China were coming to an end. Even when we lived in Shung-Li Province we always dreamt of living here in Cornwall, after visiting England on a holiday. Here is much history. Of course we Chinese have a long and noble heritage, but the old reliance on pilchards and the mining of tin is quite fascinating and I adore the myths and legends surrounding this part of Cornwall. But we have visited King Arthur's Tintagel and Land's End. Are you down here for long, Doctor?'

'Our holiday is for a fortnight,' said I. 'We are based in St Ives and stretching out from there. Mr Clark is an old friend.'

'And your Mr Holmes is so amusing when he talks of church architecture. I could listen to him for hours. Ah, but wait, Mr Tong is about to propose a toast.'

I confess I was quite smitten with Lai. She was

intelligent, eloquent, and charming company. The tone of her skin was exquisite and she seemed to me at the peak of physical condition. And yet she must have been nine and forty at least.

'Gentlemen,' said Mr Tong. 'May I propose a toast to the future restoration of St Modwen's church and the kind donation of two pounds I have received from Mr Holmes and Doctor Watson to put towards its eventual refurbishment. I trust you will enjoy the remainder of your stay in Cornwall and both Lai and I wish you a safe journey back to St Ives.' Everyone clapped. 'Mr Clark, you wish to say something?' said Mr Tong, peering over his pince-nez eye-glasses.

'I can only express how much we have enjoyed your hospitality, Mr Tong, and you too, Mrs Tong, and I hereby donate another shilling to the pot.'

* * *

Throughout our carriage ride, returning round the peninsula to St Ives, we were grim and pensive company, not because of being out of pocket, but rather because the reality was that we had been found out and caught red-handed, tampering with Mr Tong's business product. If the firework rockets did not represent in themselves the slightest concern or suspicion of criminality, the brand-new belfry bell and riveted iron font cover with its industrial chain and pulley system surely did. The new additions cast an unnerving doubt as to the true purpose of such a venture.

'Tong was seamless,' admitted Clark, tossing his cigarette aside. 'His behaviour in the light of realising

215

that his warehouse had been searched by three men of dubious intent, supposedly interested in church architecture, was impeccable. He kept his composure remarkably. I have never seen anyone quite like him.'

'The Chinese are a quite extraordinary race,' said Holmes, taking in the view of the sea. 'His control in the face of adversity, the way he offered us lunch as a means of politely extracting us from the most embarrassing of situations, Clark having been caught looking inside one of the cardboard boxes, was masterly. I take my hat off to him.'

'Lai was delightful company,' said I wistfully, recalling that graceful and yet agile way she expressed herself.

'Yes, she is the most dangerous of the pair,' said Holmes, above the clopping hooves.

'What on earth are you driving at?' said I, not liking the tone of his voice, and anxious to defend the lady's honour.

'You will have surely observed, my dear Watson, her posture, her mannerisms, her unremitting concentration. Why man, her body is honed, she is in old age younger and fitter than all of us put together. I accidentally dropped my napkin on purpose, and she caught it before it even touched the ground. Her reaction was phenomenal. My worst fears were realised for I believe her to be a proponent of ju-jitsu, of the highest dan.'

'You have lost me,' said Clark, unable to understand what my friend was referring to. I, on the other hand, knew of Holmes's long-held interest in bare knuckle fighting and martial arts.

'So her fitness regime would enable her to take part in mortal combat.'

'And win. There would be no concept of losing in the Chinese mind, once wedded to aggressive defence, or attack postures. I will give you both a demonstration. Her stance begins thus. She will in seconds take a flying kick and destroy the bridge of the nose, before following through with "*Hoi!*" and a pirouette on one foot, before finishing off with a "*Hoi!*" and a move known as "the forefinger of death". The entire routine would take a matter of seconds, and the opponent be felled to the floor, lifeless and broken.'

Clark turned very pale. He dabbed his sweating forehead with a handkerchief.

'However,' said my companion seriously, taking up his cane. 'By holding the stick in both hands and raising it above the head in a blocking motion, it might be possible to delay your demise by half a minute or so. While she pirouettes, you strike her a fatal blow to the neck. Alas, I doubt whether any of us are capable of such a swift response. Much physical training and control of the reflexes is required.'

'Well, that shines a new light on Mrs Tong, certainly,' said I.

'However, I propose we regain the upper hand, for tonight we shall return to the old church at Zennor and together, under cover of darkness, continue where we left off. Clark, do you know of a mining expert with a complete knowledge of the peninsula?'

'I will go about locating one, Mr Holmes. What

time shall we meet up? I am taking the precaution of bringing a shotgun. Mrs Tong worries me.'

'Very wise under the circumstances. To return to an earlier problem, I think we can safely assume the three bodies at Culbone's Cove were victims of an explosion that occurred during the assembly of Chinese firework rockets. The mixing of gunpowder can be a perilous affair. Ah! I see we are approaching St Ives. Half past seven it is, Mr Clark.'

* * *

Our holiday villa in St Ives proved a welcome respite from the matter concerning Mr Tong and his wife. Mrs Edenbridge, our lady help, fussed over us and prepared an excellent braised haddock for supper. At half past seven, the skies above the harbour still blue and sunny, the door bell clanged and Clark, along with a wizened old gentleman, his sparse skeletal frame clothed in a baggy white tropical suit, came out onto the balcony where Holmes was smoking a pipe, languidly staring out to sea.

'This is Mr Taylor,' said Clark, putting down an oblong-shaped packet tied up with string, containing his gun. 'He is knowledgeable on the organisation of Cornish mines and the Cornish mining economy in general. Mr Taylor, may I introduce you to Mr Sherlock Holmes, a consulting detective from London. And this is his colleague, Doctor Watson.'

'Glad to meet you, I'm sure,' said Mr Taylor, a trifle puzzled as to why he should have been asked to visit the villa. 'The weather has been...'

218

'Sunny and warm,' said Holmes, relighting his briar pipe and stretching his long legs. 'Mr Taylor, I require information and statistics.'

'Well, I am a retired mining engineer. I worked at Trethellan, West Poldice, St Austell Hills and Solgooth. The tin is still fairly profitable. Copper and lead ore remain marketable.'

'And a fellow who works a mine will enter it by what means?'

'Usually a cage operated by a rotary engine for winding the kibble and chain attached, but the shafts can be horizontal and levels approached on foot or by ladders, depending on the depth of the mine.'

'So, a cage is not necessarily required?'

'Not at all, Mr Holmes.'

'Pray, do you know of any mine operating in the vicinity of Zennor?'

'That remote village along the peninsula? I know of the old Landscomb mine, long-closed. I recall a collapse, a timberman, or binder as we call 'em, who takes care that the ground is properly secured by supports of wood and that casings and ladders in the shafts are well put in and kept in good repair, was crushed and killed. The mine working was deemed to be unstable. No one could decide what shafts should be sunk or levels driven. The mine was declared too dangerous to operate and closed down, men laid off. The unions were in agreement.'

'The Landscomb mine,' said I. 'Is there a derelict engine house somewhere on the landscape? I saw no trace of workings.'

'The best way to approach the mine today is probably shorewards, for it opens out onto the sea, and there is a man-made cave, hewn out by tin prospectors. There would be horizontal shafts still in existence, but the lower workings where the accident occurred are where the richer seams of tin are to be found. There are all sorts of tunnels and rocky, cavernous spaces below ground, if you are prepared to risk life and limb to find them.'

'Clark, a few words if I may. You shall need to telegraph the headquarters of the Cornish constabulary and alert our friends at Customs and Excise, for now we have much work to do. Watson, you'll need your service revolver, and, and Mrs Edenbridge, the loan of a couple of dark lanterns from your husband's garden shed would be most welcome.'

*   *   *

I confess, for myself and Mr Clark, the very notion of a confrontation with Mrs Tong lay heavily on our minds. Holmes did not seem unduly concerned and spent the journey emphasising the need for complete quiet and light tread of foot once inside the old Norman church. We had brought along a short stepladder that Mrs Edenbridge had found amongst cans of paint and her husband's old work tools; also a number of dark lanterns and a supply of tallow candles. Clark held on to his shotgun grimly, and as our carriage approached the outskirts of Zennor we disembarked. There was no moon, and we trudged up the hill in complete darkness. It was close to midnight and I could see no lights in either of the houses. So it seemed we were unlikely to be disturbed, provided there was no loud noise to alert the sleeping occupants.

With the use of the portable stepladder we managed to climb in through the vestry window and warily make our way into the chancel. Dark lanterns were lit and once more we were surrounded by cardboard boxes on every side. My companions took the lead and together we crept along to the carved Norman font. As was part of the plan we each got stuck in and began greasing all the mechanical parts of the pulley system copiously with tallow fat. Once Holmes was satisfied that the iron font cover should lift easily and without undue noise, Clark started to operate the mechanism. The chains began to tauten, and slowly the heavy font cover rose into the air. What was revealed was astonishing. No bowl of baptism, but a deep-driven shaft sunk many feet below ground. There was even a lamp burning down there.

'So, this is their means of entry,' said Holmes. 'Well, there's a good sturdy ladder at least. This is where they take the bales of opium to process. A remarkable achievement.'

'Opium?' whispered Clark. 'Mr Holmes, this is a serious allegation. How the devil do you countenance such a radical idea? I presumed you meant to uncover an illegal mining operation.'

'Then you presumed wrong, my dear Clark. Pray, remove the lid of the nearest box and I shall produce the proof required.'

Holmes took out his pipe knife and deftly slit open one of the Chinese firework rockets.

Gunpowder cascaded onto the flagstone floor of the nave. So there was nothing irregular there. However, digging deeper he produced a second rocket from the lower row and upon slicing the cardboard discovered a resin-like substance, solid and perfectly moulded to the firework. Peeling away the paper it became clear that the opium core was indeed being cleverly concealed in some, but not all, of the Chinese firework rockets in each box.

'So this represents a gang operation,' exclaimed the Cornish detective.

'You will recall the Chinese symbol upon the forearm of the unfortunate Oriental gentleman sprawled on the beach at Culbone's Cove. I have, as you well know, my dear Watson, an old diary in which I compile trifling oddities concerning tattoo marks. I was delighted to refresh my memory concerning a case I dealt with at the wharves at Wapping in the East End some years ago. The symbol denotes the gangland sign of that despot and crime leader known all over Europe as Chai Wang, who controls the trade of drugs in almost all major cities, and who resides in some secrecy in the docklands area of London.'

'Well, it's up to us to arrest these villains. I shall go down first, Mr Holmes. Will you be good enough to hold my shotgun while I negotiate this ladder?' said Clark.

'A tunnel chase amongst the treacherous shafts and working areas of a tin mine? My dear sir, Mr Tong should rejoice at our gross incompetence if that was to be our sole objective,' Holmes sneered. 'No, I have a much simpler and more effective means of flushing out our gang members presently employed in the processing of opium and packaging of fireworks for a shipment bound by cutter for London Docks. Watson, I think we shall throw down fifty or so boxes of fireworks, dangle down a long fuse and after lighting it, replace the font lid and retire to a safe distance behind the altar.'

'Agreed,' said I. 'The bell rope can be adapted. A length smothered in tallow and sprinkled with gunpowder for a fuse. I shall cut it now.'

'That's a good fellow. Clark, help me with the firework boxes. The blast will wake up Mr Tong, I'm sure of it.'

'And Mrs Tong.'

'We shall face that particular danger when we come to it.'

Once we had thrown enough boxes of fireworks down the shaft, the long fuse was carefully inserted and one cardboard box primed and made ready to effectively create a series of loud explosions, loud enough to alert the criminal workforce, creating a mass panic below ground. Holmes ignited the end of the makeshift fuse and once the riveted iron font cover was replaced to its closed position we ran up the aisle and flung ourselves behind the granite altar edifice, confident of the protection offered.

Not long afterwards there was a tremendous blast that shook the Norman building to its foundations and sent piles of boxes toppling to the ground.

'It is time, my dear Watson, to quit the church. We must make our way along the path down the cliffs, to the beach, where there exists the cave entrance Mr Taylor described, for that is where the mass exodus shall be heading, anxious to avoid the complete collapse of the Landscombe mine.'

Back we clambered, out of the vestry window, utilising the handy step ladder and thereafter scampering with our dark lanterns across the tall grass of the ancient churchyard towards a wrought-iron gate, whence the footpath continued along to the steep cliff steps. Alas, we ran straight into the welcoming embrace of Lai Tong, while her husband sat manning a machine-gun on stilts, a Gatling gun.

'What a pity, we must say goodbye for the last time, gentlemen. I was prepared to forgive your last misdemeanour, confident you and your friends would not return a second time to meddle with my business affairs. Alas, my patience wears thin. Lai and myself must bid you adieu, for when I press the button of this advanced machine-gun, you shall all die.'

At this instant, a curious thing happened for a megaphone being manned by an officious policeman sounded up from the water. A Navy steam launch had arrived with a contingent of customs and police officers, to cut off and arrest the rabble of workers from the beach, desperate to be clear of the dangerous mine and now fleeing from the cave mouth. 'You are under arrest!' I heard a tinny voice say.

In that second Mr Tong lost his nerve and his attention wavered. He knew his opium operation was threatened and that escape was the only option. A small, perfectly round hole appeared in his forehead, and staring blankly ahead he keeled over

224

and collapsed on top of the Gatling gun, fatally wounded. I thus trained my service revolver on Lai Tong. To my side Inspector Clark was likewise armed with his shotgun.

'If you so much as ruffle a hair on my friend's head,' said I, noticing her catlike stance and observance of the expression '*Hoi*', 'I shall put a bullet through your skull.'

My companion, who I knew was about to launch at her with his walking cane, held it in the upraised 'defensive block'. But our stalwart efforts at defeating this Oriental tigress counted for nought for she, her lithe and agile frame taut and immaculately poised, took one step backwards and then another. Still facing us, she advanced towards the horizon of the unfenced cliff edge. Lai calmly and deliberately flipped over backwards in a double somersault and was gone. A delayed splash followed. She had landed in the sea safely.

'She's damn well escaped!' ejaculated Clark, seething and throwing his shotgun to the ground in despair.

'It is partly explained by the "Honour Code",' said Holmes, taking out his cigarettes and offering us each one from the tin. 'Defeat would not be a word in Lai's vocabulary. She lives to fight another day and thus remains true to her martial arts credo. I suspect the naval steam launch will be too busily occupied marshalling the Chinese workers on the beach to pay much notice. She will swim round the coast and escape. Well, my dear Watson, dawn is breaking. I think we'd better return to our digs in St Ives. Mrs Edenbridge shall surely be preparing a breakfast of ham and eggs and I am absolutely ravenous. Inspector Clark, I trust you will keep our involvement in this case of the Landscombe mine out of the papers as a matter of principle? I look forward to a more leisurely employment of my time for the remainder of our Cornish holiday.'

13

The Fire Ritual

'A Mister Langford Lovell, the theatre manager of the Wimborne to see you, Mr Holmes.'

Mrs Hudson announced our guest and with a polite nod gently closed the door, leaving us alone with this large and genial gentleman. A sporadic dining companion at Simpsons, he was the business manager of the popular actor Charles Lemon. Together they kept the Wimborne open to full houses and had over the years put on many productions to great public acclaim. What with his considerable ability and great energy, he was normally amusing company, but on this occasion for some reason seemed out of sorts and distracted.

'Do come in, Lovell,' said Holmes, giving up his own chair. 'Here, come and sit by the fire. It is drearily damp outside.'

'Well,' said I, 'Lemon's Falstaff has never been bettered. Is Charles fit and well?'

'Oh yes, thank you, Doctor Watson. He is in perfect health and well rested after his latest triumph.'

Triumph! The business manager's agitated state indicated otherwise. Had the critics panned Lemon's latest performance? Had theatre audiences crashed?

I had not consulted the review pages inside *The Times* for some weeks, but as it turned out Langford Lovell had not ventured to our Baker Street lodgings to sob on Holmes's shoulder.

He lit a cheroot with a vesta from his waistcoat pocket.

'I have come here, Mr Holmes, on behalf of a titled lady. There is some discretion required at this juncture, gentlemen.'

We both nodded gravely and he continued.

'The lady's mind has become quite deranged on account of a continued and relentless persecution, by a person or group unknown, possibly some secret society. The most recent shocking episode in this shameful affair took place yesterday evening: a fire ritual. Lord Asprey is quite beside himself with worry, as indeed are we all. His poor darling wife has taken to her bed.'

'A fire ritual?' said I. 'Is that not an occult practice? The use of flames and diabolical symbols of necromancy to invoke the Devil?'

'I fear that is the case, Doctor Watson. But it is the lady's fragile state of mind that concerns me most,' said he, puffing the more earnestly on his cheroot.

'Of course, Lovell,' ejaculated Holmes, seizing his oily black clay from the mantelpiece and filling it with tobacco. 'And it is at Shaddrick Hall, the country seat of Lord Asprey, that this fire ritual took place, I take it?'

'Absolutely. Listen Holmes, Lord and Lady Asprey are very dear to us. I informed his lordship of your considerable reputation as a consulting detective and at Charles Lemon's specific request I set off for your rooms at Baker Street this morning. The latest development concerns a number of threatening letters Lady Asprey has received over the last week from an infamous correspondent by the name of Diablo. I am begging you, Sir, to intervene.'

'My dear Lovell,' said Holmes, puffing on his pipe. 'I and Doctor Watson would be only too delighted to be of some assistance. The case intrigues me. Halloa, what's that you're concealing in your pocket? Theatre tickets? Why, I have not yet solved the crime,' chuckled my companion. 'Are they balcony seats or front row?'

The theatre manager did not seem particularly amused by Holmes's attempt to lighten the mood.

'I shall send a telegram to Lord Asprey immediately, to inform him of your involvement. The envelope I have here contains *train* tickets and directions to his stately home. Time is of the essence, Mr Holmes.'

'Well,' said my companion, poking about the grate and relighting his pipe from a burning coal held betwixt fireside tongs, 'let us consult Bradshaw's, for we have a long train journey ahead, and the southern counties of England have need of us, Watson.'

* * *

We travelled first to Tunbridge Wells and, after changing trains, eventually alighted upon a little light railway that runs from the town of Tenterden along the Rother Valley. Below Bodiam is Ewhurst and a little further east lies Lallington. A branch line journey is always a delight. I smoked my pipe contentedly, admiring the passing scenery, the snug villages and hamlets, the trees resplendent in the vivid bronze, rusty reds and yellow hues of autumn, the arable land broken only by hedgerows bursting with wild fruits and berries, a sure sign of a hard winter to come. My companion meanwhile sat opposite smoking a cigarette, buried in the pages of *The Times*, only occasionally glancing up from his paper to consider the view.

We were assured by the old porter at Lallington station that it was only a brief trudge of a half mile or so and it would not take us long to reach the gates of Shaddrick Hall, a stately home that indeed could be glimpsed from the branch line platform. We could see imposing chimneys, a leaded roof of an agreeable green hue resembling old copper, and a turreted clock tower wreathed in vapours of autumnal mist.

What struck me as we approached along the avenue of pollarded limes and chestnuts was the sheer grandeur of the place. It was an elegant period building with its ample windows, perfect proportions and aesthetic satisfaction that often attends the shape of such a house. Here was one of the grand houses of Georgian England, with a fountain, an obelisk, Grecian follies and unrobed statues of nymphs and satyrs only adding to the pleasure.

Lord Asprey greeted us on the portico and led us into the house. He was a charming fellow, a fine, upstanding gentleman who attended the House of Westminster and championed the rights of the poor, arguing the case for reform. 'Langford and

Charles Lemon are dear friends,' he began. 'We meet occasionally at the Athenaeum Club and you are no doubt aware that her ladyship and I are patrons of the Wimborne Theatre.'

'How is your wife keeping?' I asked.

'This dreadful business of the fire ritual has left a dark stain upon our house, Doctor Watson. My wife has taken to her bed.'

'Well, firstly,' said Holmes, 'is there a symbol of the occult involved?'

'Over here, gentlemen,' said he, leading us across the wide expanse of Persian carpet to the grand fireplace, which was an imposing edifice, built of purest white Carrara marble with the Aspreys' coat of arms at its centre and surmounted by a wide mantelpiece on which stood Chinese vases and a pair of gigantic candlesticks.

The answer was plain to see, for there in the grate, amongst a heap of grey ash, lay a tiny skull.

'There was no intruder that night, Mr Holmes, no maid or servant had visited the room save for Mrs Booth, our head housekeeper, who assures me all was exactly as it should be. The fireplace was untampered with, the coals recently lit, for her ladyship often prefers to come in here after formal dinner to quietly read her novels.'

'May I inspect the fireplace?' said Holmes, getting down on his knees and examining the curious object with his magnifying lens. Thereafter, he snatched the skull and held it up to the light of the window like Hamlet.

'Watson,' said he, 'is this the skull of a small ape, a langur monkey for instance?'

I held it carefully in my hand, examining its shape and the position of the cavities. There could only be one logical explanation.

'It is human,' said I. 'The cranium, jawbone and eye sockets are consistent with those of a child between the ages of six and ten.' At this news, Lord Asprey appeared a trifle unsteady on his feet. He was led over to the sofa by Mrs Booth, who fussed over him and poured a glass of water from a carafe upon the sideboard.

'Then it is even worse than we feared, for the skull is surely the result of some sacrificial offering,' said Asprey despairingly.

Holmes kept his voice calm and delivered a measured response. 'Let us at this early juncture not presume the worst, but rather keep a balanced view upon the subject.' He got up and dusted himself down. 'The threatening letters, if you please.'

Whilst I gazed beyond the windows towards Lallington, a tiny village encompassed by the estate, its church presently shrouded in mist, Lord Asprey fetched a bundle of envelopes from a French escritoire, and passed them to my companion.

'These letters are not my primary concern. I am at present more interested in your household accounts. Are your ledgers kept with your estate manager at his office? I do not wish to cause undue disturbance to his working arrangements, but I should like to examine the ledgers in minute detail.'

'Well Mr Holmes, the bulk of the accounts ledgers are kept in my library. They go back many years, some as early as the eighteenth century. There is quite a history of household business contained in them, or is it more recent figures you are after? Those Wilson does keep in his office.'

'The library stock will do for now, thank you Lord Asprey,' said Holmes.

Mrs Booth hurried across and whispered in his lordship's ear.

'Well, I am going to hand you over to Mrs Booth, my redoubtable head housekeeper, whom I have personally requested should show you round the house and familiarise you with the various rooms. I shall ring for a servant to prepare the library and take down the ledgers for your perusal from the bookshelves.'

* * *

Mrs Booth, a most charming and vivacious head housekeeper, was a positive fund of knowledge when it came to discussing every aspect of the house, from the many treasures and valuable paintings on display to the workings of below-stairs, in which Holmes seemed particularly interested. After a shortened tour she directed us to the library, and sat us down at a long oak table, where I was glad to see a tray of cold meats and other delicacies. I confess I was in need of sustenance after our long train journey, as indeed was Holmes, who attacked his meal with a vigorous appetite. Then he began a study of the ancient leather-bound account books. He started with Volume 1 and swiftly progressed to Volume 2. I observed the entries were neatly written in much-faded brown and red ink. Running his long finger up and down the columns of figures, Holmes examined each page of vellum parchment minutely with his magnifying lens.

Some time later, the light outside had started to fade and the steadily ticking clock upon the mantelpiece struck the hour. Mrs Booth was busy lighting each oil lamp in turn with a taper, allowing a tranquil glow to settle on the library. Upon the last resonating chime, he who had been preoccupied by ledger upon ledger of household accounts, leapt up from his Tudor oak chair and flung his magnifying lens across the room.

'I see it, Watson. I have solved the mystery. Now I realise my judgement is sound and that for the very first time the fire ritual can be properly explained. Mrs Booth, would you be good enough to arrange a meeting in his lordship's study? Pray inform Lady Asprey of the proceedings. Watson, have you some strong tobacco handy? For I have smoked my own supply in considering this problem.'

* * *

We all assembled in the study a little before half past five. Lady Asprey had come downstairs and for the first time I saw what a strikingly beautiful woman she was, but she presented a languid, other-worldly disposition, a complete indifference to her surroundings, wholly consistent with regular doses of laudanum being prescribed by her family physician.

'Lady Asprey, I can assure you the fire ritual has nothing to do with either a diabolical secret society of Freemasons, or the occultists. It involves a great tragedy certainly, but from olden times. Steel yourself, for what I am about to relate concerns a brutal murder certainly, but firstly let me put your mind at rest concerning the skull. Do you recall the autumnal gales of the last week? Mrs Booth commented on their severity and said that some of the farm cottages had been damaged, roof tiles awry, chimney pots toppled over at Lallington and so forth.'

'Oh Mr Holmes, how the wind howled. The windows of the house were battened up, some trees in the park were felled,' she answered.

'Precisely, and it was the severe autumnal gales that ravaged Surrey and Sussex which were responsible for dislodging the skull so that due to the forces of gravity it tumbled down the chimney and landed squarely in the grate, just prior to your entering the sitting room to read one of your novels. The intense heat of the cheery fire was of course responsible for its unearthly red glow. What a fright it must have been to encounter such a macabre object, the visions of the occult being firmly etched in the subconscious.

'The crux of this puzzling case is a crime long forgotten, the perpetrator being a master chimney-sweep by the name of Thomas Packham, who lived in Tenterden, close to the Surrey border. He attended this house on March the first, 1776. In those distant times there were no long-poled brushes with which today we are all familiar. Instead, the chimney-sweep would employ climbing boys, mere urchins purchased from destitute mothers for gin money, and paid a pittance to perform the most dirty and dangerous tasks, including climbing barefoot up the inner flues and gigantic chimney stacks of great stately homes, such as Shaddrick Hall. The victim, the young child, is nameless. We know nothing about his grim and short life and yet we have a perfect glimpse of his dramatic and untimely death, for at some stage of climbing the flues and chimneys to the living room, an avalanche of soot became dislodged and the child would have become asphyxiated, buried beneath its mass and smothered to death.

'But the examination of the facts does not end here, for the master chimney-sweep, Thomas Packham, is transformed from negligent employer to murderer most foul, for he did not once try to save the boy's life and instead of demanding the wall in that part of the house should be knocked down and a way found to rescue and extricate the poor child, he decided his reputation was of more importance and the prospect of being charged in a court of law for negligent work practices abhorrent. He thus simply left the unconscious urchin and walked away with his fee – two shillings – for cleaning flues and chimneys. The child's skull is but a part of an entire skeleton lodged fast in the vast chimney flue for centuries.

'Now let us address the problem of the threatening letters. The culprit I deduce from talking to the servants, Mrs Booth in particular, is Mason. The vindictive missives represent the mere psychotic ramblings of a dismissed servant bearing a considerable grudge. For example: *Your Ladyship is a bad egg. Soon you will be privy to my righteous wrath and feel the full force of his vengeance. Nowhere is safe. Yours Diablo.*

'Diablo is of course the literary alias of Mason, shortly to be arrested by the West Sussex division of police on account of inky fingerprints, the thumb and forefinger in particular, discovered on both letters and envelopes caused by the clumsy use of a pen with a scratchy, square nib. The postmarks upon each envelope are from Horsham, the post office no doubt being close to his present lodgings.'

'Mason?' uttered Lady Asprey. 'Why, that cur should have been horsewhipped. He was dismissed a fortnight past on suspicion of stealing a silver cigar case belonging to my husband. His references were impeccable, from a Lady Billington.'

'And entirely fabricated,' said Holmes. 'You will be well rid of him.'

14

Mrs Munn's Tea Caddy

One autumn Sherlock Holmes received a most amusing correspondence addressed to our lodgings in Baker Street. I cannot raise this account to the heady heights of great literature, but for sheer mirth it cannot be bettered.

I recall upon that memorable morning Mrs Hudson was about to consign the aforementioned note to the flames of a roaring fire when Holmes, for some reason, snatched the piece of curling paper, saving it from a fiery end. I confess, each of us in the room had read it in turn and chuckled accordingly.

Mrs Hudson, wiping her eyes, still disbelieving the contents, perched on the corner of Holmes's armchair.

'Oh, do read it out loud,' she implored my companion before getting up to clear away the breakfast things.

'Our valiant correspondent deserves better,' said he.

Dear Mr Sherlock Holmes,
I am Mrs Munn of Clapham Terrace, a person of little consequence, a tiny ant crawling about

this great metropolis of ours. A neighbour of mine suggested I might specifically contact you on account of my tea caddy, which recently has taken up a habit of moving about the shelf when I am not looking. It moves of its own accord, when it wants. It annoys me when it wants. Please visit me at Clapham and I shall elaborate further upon the subject of poltergeists. I must forewarn you that I am a committed 'believer' and keen admirer of Florrie Sitwell, the medium.

'A spiritualist,' I remarked, sipping the last dregs of my coffee, thereafter reaching for my pipe and matches.

'Yes indeed, Watson, and yet, you know I think I'll take her up on the offer. The last case concerning the railway murder has left me a trifle out of sorts and in need of honest amusement. Come Watson, where's Bradshaw's? We shall take a train from Victoria to Clapham Junction and walk to the terrace from there. Expect us to return to Baker Street at around noon, Mrs Hudson. I dare say this will end in complete farce, but the exercise will do us both good.'

We took a cab to Victoria Station. A foul yellow fog blanketed the metropolis all the while the hansom rattled along. I peered at the dun-coloured houses, the gloom of the fog occasionally penetrated by the hazy glow of carriage lamps, else the lighted shop fronts made ethereal and blurred by the persistent poisonous and stifling atmosphere.

From Clapham Junction we walked briskly to

No. 5 The Terrace, a red-brick semi-detached house in a row of others.

Sitting by a shaded budgie cage, Mrs Munn scrutinised us from behind half-closed lids. 'You are neither of you "believers", I take it?'

'On the contrary Mrs Munn, we are both most sympathetic to the spiritualist cause. I have no reason to doubt your poltergeist inhabiting the cupboard of your warm and commodious kitchen here in Clapham.'

'The tea caddy, Mr Holmes.'

'Of course, Mrs Munn.'

'It moved, it moved when I was not looking.'

'And emptied itself,' said I, barely able to restrain from laughing out loud, causing untold offence to the dear lady.

'Emptied itself and scattered tea leaves upon the kitchen floor. All without human interference,' said she, listening intently to the budgie fluttering its wings in the cage.

'Remarkable,' ejaculated Holmes, taking the whole matter very seriously. 'Pray tell me, Mrs Munn, when last did the poltergeist strike?'

'Twas this morning, my budgie was tweeting, I had my back turned and the tea caddy flew sir, of its own accord, from one side of my kitchen to the other, knocking over an egg cup and damaging the gloss-work of my window sill. See the chipped board?'

'The tea caddy is nothing remarkable,' said I, examining the object. 'It is not antique or of great value. Its shape corresponds to many other printed tin tea receptacles. Here Holmes, the painted

241

Japanese garden, geisha ladies with their feet bound. Mrs Hudson owns one similar.'

'And yet it is somehow possessed.'

'Indeed Mr Holmes, we "believers" would infer an evil poltergeist is responsible. I have discussed the matter with Mr Lincoln at our spiritualist church and he is of the same mind.'

'We can thus eliminate the tea caddy itself, for it has been in your possession for many years, Mrs Munn, and there has been no trouble. I therefore propose it is the latest batch of tea leaves we must focus our energies upon. The brand?'

'Twiggings Dividend tea, Sir.'

'You did not throw away the packet?'

'I did not sir. I have it here in the drawer.'

'Excellent. Well Mrs Munn, leave the matter with myself and Doctor Watson here. We shall see ourselves out.'

We bid Mrs Munn good day and departed The Terrace in jovial spirits which even the gloom of a November fog could not dispel.

The next stage was simplicity itself, for my companion paused beneath a wrought-iron street lamp, took out his magnifying lens and closely examined the small print on the tea packet. Peering over his shoulder, I noted an address:

Twiggings Imperial Tea Ltd
Importer and Exporter
City Wharf
Castle Street
E.C.1

From Clapham Junction we took the next train to London Bridge, the first-class compartment allowing us a respite from the chilly, damp air and the impenetrable fog that had for many days hampered visibility, making walking and crossing roads a hazardous affair. But the fog brought with it a further nuisance, for prior to our expedition to Mrs Munn's house, I had ventured to the tobacconist for cigarettes, only to observe my overcoat and hat dotted with smuts of coal ash. I well recall the smelly steam underground railway in '61 that ran a branch up to St Johns Wood from Baker Street, which left similar deposits.

We took a cab to the office of Twiggings Imperial Tea Ltd. and, dwarfed by the entrance hall, were allowed to take our seats and await an interview with L. Smith, the Chairman, who proved knowledgeable on all aspects of tea production, although more concerned with the control and quality of each individual packet of Twiggings Dividend Tea. He seemed anyhow to take the poltergeist association in good humour, perhaps believing us to be a couple of harmless eccentrics.

Holmes presented Mr Smith with the empty packet Mrs Munn had so wisely decided to save and in our presence he carefully parcelled this up, together with a note indicating its own unique reference number, promising he would contact us when he had heard back from the Indian plantation from whence the tea leaves originally came, for even the tea chest in which they were exported was stamped with a number and could be traced.

Why, the reader may ask, were we treated to such

equanimity, the frivolous nature of Mrs Munn's tea caddy seemingly swept aside and ignored? Because the reputation of Mr Sherlock Holmes in the city as a consulting detective of great renown preceded him and opened many doors. We were even offered lunch and fine cigars in the wood-panelled board room of that same establishment and passed a very happy hour or two with the Chairman before returning to our rooms in Baker Street.

It was a fortnight later before we heard any more concerning the tea leaves. A letter arrived one morning post-marked E.C.1 and its contents proved remarkable. I had been at the time sat over by the roaring fire perusing the latest medical advances in science in my copy of *The Lancet*. Holmes called Mrs Hudson and together we marvelled at what was revealed in the letter.

India Office, 209

Greetings Shri Chairman Namaste Sahib.

A great many things have come to light since your last esteemed epistle arrived here at our blending and packing plant in Nagpur, at the end of August. It appears a Pakistani employee, by the name of Musaffadi, died last year of old age and was cremated on the estate. Oh, Lord Krishna, protect our souls, for beneath the hut where once he slept, was later uncovered the remains of, at least, seven persons (four of them women) – all have since been identified as casual tea pickers from a nearby plantation, each of whom it was said must have been strangled with a silk scarf.

Oh what infamy: for discovered amongst Musaffadi's meagre belongings was a bronze cast of the evil goddess Kali. Sahib Radley Wilberforce, our Old Etonian manager, duly informed the police. Alas, what can the police do now – absolutely nothing.

Regarding the other interesting point raised in your letter, I can only dare to surmise that certain of the murderous devil's cremated remains blown across the estate by the winds prior to the monsoon inadvertently landed upon one of our stock-piles and thence the tea leaves, polluted by Musaffadi's ashes and packed in chests, found their way across the oceans of the world to Great Britain.

Perhaps this can explain why the poor white woman of which Mr Holmes speaks so eloquently was prey to such supernatural forces – no!

Yours humbly, KHARADI (Foreman), TWIGGINGS IMPERIAL BLENDING AND PACKING PLANT, NAGPUR PROVINCE.

That afternoon we set off to Mrs Munn's house. The fog had lifted briefly, allowing a hazy glimmer of sunshine to shine through. When we arrived, the front door had been left open.

'My dear Mrs Munn, I am a harbinger bearing glad tidings,' shouted Holmes upon entering the terrace, full of bonhomie. With a flourish he slung his top hat upon the hall stand, glanced briefly in the mirror and continued along the hall to Mrs Munn's sitting room. She was sat as before in her chintz-covered chair, the black cloth still draped over the cage and the budgerigar hidden from view. When on earth does she remove the cloth, I wondered. Was the poor little bird always confined to the dark? However, it seemed to be merrily cheeping and I heard the flutter of tiny wings.

Over a fresh pot of tea, Mrs Munn was presented with the letter from the company office. Her beady eyes missed nothing.

'This explains everything,' she murmured approvingly.

Before we left Mrs Munn's house, she seized Holmes's hand and, palm upwards, gave him a reading. I suspected this was her way of showing gratitude for all he had done.

'This very week you shall hear from a sensitive known as Mr Pearce Chope. He and I are linked, you see, gentlemen. An invisible thread. One London spiritualist church to another. He will take you on a journey, help you "believe", as I do, in the presence of the spirit world. Help you attain the higher planes of existence we all aspire to.'

'Pearce Chope,' said I, suddenly anxious to leave, feeling a sudden chill enter the room, realising for the first time the cover on the bird cage had of its own accord slipped to the floor and that the budgerigar staring inquisitively at me from its dowel perch was in fact clockwork.

* * *

3 Horsebury Row, Camden

Dear Sir,

Meet me at my Camden lodgings on Thursday at seven o'clock. I have good news, Mr Holmes. Mrs Munn speaks well of you. Together we shall go upon an amazing journey. Bring your companion Doctor Watson. We are believers together.

Yours truly,

Pearce Chope

Pearce Chope was a wiry, cadaverous individual of, I should say, five and thirty, whose ill-fitting clothes hung off him like a tent. Greying temples, cold black eyes, a thin moustache and an unsmiling mouth did not prepossess him of much warmth or human kindness but he was friendly enough.

At that time Chope had digs situated in a fairly drab part of London, a third-floor flat. Gaze out of the window and you could see the Underground station just down the road from where he lived.

Mr Chope invited us in for supper. The meal was plain bachelor fare, a couple of stringy chops, followed afterwards by canned suet pudding embellished with lumpy custard. Supper finished, we retired to the sitting room where we smoked our cigarettes and chatted amiably.

That night it was foggy outside. We sat huddled over the coal fire. The tiny room seemed to reflect Mr Chope's indifference to the comforts of material living: bland lino, faded flock wallpaper, in one corner a cupboard with a few volumes on the subject of spiritualism.

'I will fetch us a glass of port each,' said he, getting up from his worn-out armchair with its greasy, shiny headrest. 'I have a bottle of Cockburn's at the back of my cupboard that will do nicely.' Warming his hands in front of the feeble, flickering coal fire that smoked badly he proposed the following diversion.

'Gentlemen, you upon whom I count as true friends, I propose that tonight we take a journey on the Underground railway.'

'Well, pray, what is our destination, Mr Chope?' asked Holmes.

'Archway Station, Sir.'

Sherlock Holmes rubbed the ridge of his beaky nose with a long forefinger and elaborated. 'Archway Station is upon the Northern Line, not so many stops from Camden. Southbound one travels from Camden Town to Kentish Town, Tufnell Park and thereafter Archway. I should say the abrupt curves in the track make the cars jolt and sway without warning. The long dark tunnels are musty and airless, altogether a most dreary and depressing ride. I should on the whole prefer the Metropolitan or Circle Line. What say you, my dear Watson?'

'As long as it's not that smelly, smoky old branch up to St Johns Wood I am perfectly happy to comply,' said I, finishing my port.

After putting on our hats and coats we left Chope's flat and walked briskly through the fog in the direction of the Underground, the old tenements of Camden lamplit and dismal, a procession of omnibuses and carriages moving at a snail's pace alongside the kerb.

What on earth was the purpose of dragging us out on a foggy night to ride the subterranean railway? For myself, I fancied we were about to meet some psychic friend of his, active at a spiritualist church in north London. Holmes, I am sure, was of the same opinion.

The steady rhythm of the Underground cars nulled my thoughts. I perceived my own dour reflection in the glass of the compartment window. Kentish Town and the sudden garish yellow lights temporarily broke the spell. A few passengers alighted and I perceived that Holmes, whose face seemed to shiver and change shape like elastic, sat absently studying the Hacks cough lozenge advertisement above Chope's head. 'The sensitive' himself had his eyes closed, lost in some deep trance.

At Archway, we left the stuffy cars and proceeded towards the lifts which conveyed passengers to the surface. Breathing in the dry, ozonified atmosphere, Chope seized my arm and indicated we should instead walk along the platform to the tiled entrance leading to the northbound line. I confess at this juncture I felt a trifle unsteady on my legs and was finding it increasingly difficult to keep hold of reality.

'Are we to travel back to Camden so soon?' asked Holmes.

'Be still sir,' snapped Chope, 'we are in the presence of a restless spirit who must ride the hellish treadmill for eternity. Now Doctor Watson, and you Mr Holmes, look that way, where I am pointing – the tunnel mouth!'

A train approached. The rushing of fetid air from the tunnel mouth and the ringing of the rail acted like a moth to a flame to a poor disturbed fellow who, discarding his top hat, dived off the northbound platform directly in the path of the oncoming train.

'Guard!' I shouted, a little of the numbness in my face and hands dissipating. 'A man has jumped in front of the train.'

'Come Watson,' I heard Sherlock Holmes's stern voice speaking to me as from a great distance, as if partially underwater. 'No one has jumped. You have suffered a vision.'

My friend then admonished Chope in the strongest terms. 'You are a charlatan, Mr Chope. Your cheap opiate induced visions. Oh yes, I recognise the symptoms well enough. Fortunately I did not drink your glass of Cockburn's port laced with laudanum. Count yourself lucky I do not break every bone in your body for what you have just subjected Doctor Watson to. Come, dear fellow, to the lift. You shall shortly have all the fresh air you require. Mr Chope, I trust we will not be seeing each other again and neither will you contact my Baker Street address by any means or send psychic literature. This represents closure, an end to our association. Goodnight.'

What an odd thing it was to be stood upon Archway station in an altered state such as that. As a postscript, unlike Holmes, I myself bore Mr Chope no ill feelings. The journey had been a positive one. I believe 'the sensitive' merely used an opiate as a means of opening my mind to the presence of the spirit world, the habitation of ghosts and phantoms. The ghost of the gentleman wearing the top hat continues to haunt Archway station to this day.

I must also relate it was with great sadness that some years later I learnt in *The Times* obituary column of the passing of Pearce Chope, who had himself succumbed to suicidal tendencies and leapt under a train at Honor Oak Park.

Acknowledgements

Special thanks go to my editor, Jon Ingoldby, for his helpful suggestions and improvements to the text, and to Carol Biss, Joanna Bentley and Janet Wrench at Book Guild Publishing for their encouragement and enthusiasm for the project. I should also like to thank Olivia Guest at Jonathan Clowes Ltd Literary Agents, and Amanda Payne for all her help and the staff at my local library for assisting me with the gathering of research material.